Inheriting Trouble

WENDY MAY ANDREWS

Sparrow Ink
www.sparrowdeck.com

This is a work of fiction. Names, characters, places, and incidents are a product of the author's imagination. Any resemblance to actual persons, events, or locales is entirely coincidental.

ISBN - 978-1-989634-06-6

www.wendymayandrews.com

The inheritance was meant to better her life, not muddle it.

Georgia Holton, wellborn but nearly penniless, is best friends with one of the Earl of Sherton's five daughters. When she is invited to accompany her friend for two weeks of the Season, Georgia jumps at the opportunity to have a little adventure away from her small village.

The Earl of Crossley is handsome, wealthy, widowed, and jaded. He has no intention of courting any of this Season's debutantes. After all, every woman he's ever known has been dishonest, including his late wife. But when a chance encounter throws him into contact with the Sherton ladies and their lovely friend, he can't help being drawn to Georgia's beauty and endearing personality.

When confusion about Georgia's small inheritance becomes known, a sense of obligation to right a wrong forces the earl and Georgia into close association.

But is she really different from any of the other women, or does she have an ulterior motive?

And can Georgia even consider getting close to a man from High Society, when all she wants is to return to her simple village life?

Sparks fly between these two, but it will take forgiveness and understanding on both their parts to reach a happily ever after.

Dedication

Once again, there's a strong theme of friendship in this book. I believe friendships are the cornerstone of a happy life. In this story, communication is key to working out the best possible future for all involved. This is a weakness for many people (including me) so I'm dedicating this book to all those who are struggling to improve their relationships with better communication. When you figure it out, message me to tell me how ;-)

Acknowledgements

Marlene, Suzanne, Alfred, Monique, and Christina: Thank you for taking the time and effort to help me work out the holes in early drafts of this story. Your loving kindness in my writing journey means the world to me.

Editing – Julie Sherwood, you are a dream to work with. You make my stories better and are generous with your time. Any errors remaining are the fault of the author.

Cover – Les at German Creative was a marvel.

Hubby – Mr. Andrews, you have been with me every step of the way. Thank you for supporting me, following along with my characters' adventures, helping me with the business side of things, and being the best partner there is. We'll conquer this thing yet.

Chapter One

Spring 1805

Georgia had to exert every ounce of her will in order to remain still. Her discomfort in the middle of the backward facing seat seemed to increase as the carriage finally rolled into London. Every particle of her person wanted to press itself against the window and gaze about. But it would not do to draw the attention of Lady Sherton.

Lady Sherton had been in fine form from the moment they had set foot in the carriage that morning. She had expressed displeasure over everything she encountered, which made Georgia decidedly nervous. She could not bear it if the countess took it into her head that Georgia was excess baggage and sent her back to Sherton. Georgia was quite well aware that she was only there on sufferance, based on the begging of her dear friend, the countess's third daughter, Lady Vigilia, who had assured her mother that she absolutely could not bear to come up to London without Georgia's company. Lady Sherton had agreed that Georgia could accompany them for two weeks. She had been heard to mutter, 'What can it matter with the first two still to marry off, having a friend to occupy her might keep her from under foot.'

The greenery flashing by the windows had given way to densely constructed buildings. Georgia was fascinated by it all. She had never been outside their small village. Not in body anyway. Her imagination had allowed her to travel through the pages of well-written books, but from what little she could see from her vantage point, her imagination hadn't done London justice. She truly hoped Vicky would be willing to go wandering with her because she was itching to see the city up close.

Lady Vigilia, Vicky to her friends, must have sensed Georgia's suppressed frustration over the poor visibility as she cast her a sympathetic glance. She refrained from comment, though, as her sister had just hissed, "There he is! Lord Crossley! He is looking particularly fine this afternoon."

"Hilaria Sherton, do not be so ill bred," reprimanded her vigilant mother.

Rosabel, the oldest of the Sherton sisters, looked at Hilaria with laughter dancing in her eyes. "You mustn't say such things out loud, Hil, but, of course, one cannot help but think them."

Lady Sherton shot her eldest daughter a reproving glance but didn't bother to contradict her. Georgia thought she might have seen the woman's lips twitch but dismissed the suspicion, as she doubted the countess found anything amusing. She then quickly reprimanded herself for the uncharitable thought; she ought to be more positive about the lady, seeing as she was allowing Georgia to accompany them to Town even though she was rather beneath her notice socially speaking.

Georgia tried not to sigh audibly over that thought. She really wasn't beyond the pale. But she was far from being an earl's daughter, that was for certain. And since she qualified for the Byram Bequest, it was obvious that her circumstances were less than ideal. But she did qualify and now had a dowry of ten pounds. She could feel her lips forming a soft smile as she thought of dear Mr. Byram and his generous Will. She was quite well aware that ten pounds was paltry next to the dowry the Sherton girls had, but for her it would make all the difference. After she had this brief holiday with Vicky, she would return to their village and find some kind shopkeeper to marry, and she would be able to ensure a secure, well-fed future for her siblings.

Georgia thought back to when she and Lady Vigilia had been making their plans. Georgia never thought of her dearest friend with her proper name, but she supposed she ought to become more used to it. It wouldn't do to be calling her Vicky as they went amongst the *ton*. Just the thought of Lady Sherton's face if she were to overhear it made Georgia fight another fit of giggles.

"Are you absolutely certain your mother won't mind me accompanying you? She doesn't seem to care much for your association with someone from the village."

Vicky rolled her eyes. "She doesn't mean you when she says that. You're gentry."

"But not landed gentry."

Vicky wrinkled her nose in reply. "Now who's being the snobbish one?"

Georgia laughed. "I don't really care about my status except for the awkward place it leaves me in trying to provide for my brothers and sisters. I wish I could become a governess, but I'm not certain my education would be considered sufficient to provide for noble youngsters. Besides the fact that I couldn't really leave my own youngsters behind."

"You could try to find a husband while you're with me in London," Vicky pointed out.

"Do you really think two weeks is long enough to find a husband, Vick?"

Vicky shrugged. "Many betrothals are announced that quickly."

Georgia had meant her question to be rhetorical. She had no intention of aligning herself with a member of High Society. She didn't have an opportunity to point this out, however, before Vicky continued.

"And you could always stay longer. I certainly have no desire for you to leave after a mere fortnight. The fun will have barely begun by then."

"You know I can hardly leave my father and the children to their own devices for long. Two weeks is already longer than I'm comfortable with."

Vicky shook her head. "You are an unnatural girl, Georgia Holton."

Georgia chuckled over her friend's words. "I think you might have it the wrong way around, Vick. You don't understand since you're the exact middle of five sisters, and you still have both your parents, besides being wealthy and all the rest. If you were in my shoes, you'd do the same. I'm sure of it."

Vicky looked sceptical but changed the subject.

"Are you any further ahead in your thoughts on which of the available village men you think you'll choose to marry when you come back?"

Georgia sighed as the previous laughter drained from her. She shook her head. "I've known them all since I was born, Vick, which makes it strange to consider marrying any of them. And the fact that none of them even considered me of interest until we found out I would be eligible for the Bequest, doesn't endear any of them further to me."

"I'm sure," Vicky murmured.

Georgia laughed again. "I know ten pounds still seems paltry to you, but for me, it's going to make all the difference in how I can make life better for Susan, Marianne, and Drew. With Gregory enlisted, I don't have to worry about providing for him, but with my father's failing health, I need to be sure I can keep food on the table for the little ones. And I would rather die than allow my brothers go to work in the mines. Surely marrying one of the village men will be better than death."

Vicky grinned over Georgia's droll tone. "I dearly hope so. But I still think you should at least keep your mind open to the possibility of making a match while you're in Town, George. There are some fine gentlemen who would be thrilled to have you."

Georgia returned Vicky's wide smile. "Don't you try to bamboozle me, Vigilia Sherton. I've been listening to you and your sisters discuss the gentlemen of the ton *for years. I am well aware of the fact that any man who would be willing to take me and my siblings on must have a passel of children of his own needing care, and he'd rather take on a wife than hire a governess."*

"Well didn't you just get finished saying you wish you could become a governess?"

Georgia dissolved into laughter over her friend's question.

"Never mind about this, now tell me again about the gowns. You know I only have one gown that would be even remotely acceptable for Society."

"You always look perfectly fine, George, but none of our everyday clothes are good enough for the events of the Season. But Bel and Hil have both said they're willing to let you have some of their older gowns, and you can wear anything of mine that you'd like, so you needn't worry at all about what you'll wear. We're all pretty much the same size, and one of the maids will be able to easily make any slight adjustments that might be needed."

"I can hardly believe your sisters are being so generous. They never seem to be anything above lukewarm towards my presence."

Vicky laughed again. "You know they love you almost like an extra sister," she began. "But in all honesty, I think they found me excessively annoying last year and expect having you along will keep me out of their affairs."

Georgia smiled. "That makes much more sense. But I still can't believe the countess doesn't mind having me along."

"She agrees with my sisters in this matter. And since you are more likely to keep me out of trouble than lead me into it, she doesn't mind at all. Papa even said you are to have pin money while we're in Town."

"Oh no, I absolutely couldn't accept. It's enough that you are all being so generous already."

Vicky didn't press the subject, much to Georgia's relief.

Georgia returned to the present with a blink of her eyes. As she glanced out the window once more it crossed her mind to wonder if her experiences in London might spoil her for the simple future before her. She hardened her resolve. Her future was already settled. This was just a short vacation for her from reality, and she was going to enjoy every last second of it. Starting now, she thought as she focused on the fascinating scene passing by the window. The slowing traffic allowed her a better view, but it was hard for her to take it all in and harder still to contain her excitement. Even the more experienced young ladies in the carriage couldn't maintain their façade of ennui.

Rosabel, the oldest Sherton sister, nearly bounced in her seat. "This is going to be my Season, Mama, I can just feel it. The lord of my dreams is going to sweep me off my feet and away to his estate where I shall live happily ever after."

Her younger sister, Hilaria, Latin for cheerful, was not aptly named, which she quickly revealed as she sneered at her sister's words. "What do you expect to be different about this year from last? Nothing much about you has changed."

Rosabel ignored her sister's negativity and smiled benignly out the window. Looking at her, Georgia couldn't imagine why the beautiful young woman hadn't been swept away, as she said, in her first Season, let alone allowing a few to go by. She was beautiful, well bred, well dowered, and the daughter of an old, aristocratic family. If she couldn't find a good match there wasn't any hope for anyone else, Georgia thought with wonder. Her silent question was answered when Lady Sherton reprimanded Hilaria.

"Your sister is not to be criticized for being particular about her choice. She is determined to find joy in her marriage, and I cannot say that is a bad thing." Although from her tone, Lady Sherton didn't sound completely convinced.

"Well, it would be so much easier for the rest of us if she would hurry up and make her choice. No one will even look at me while she is still available," Hilaria grumbled.

"Perhaps if you tried to be a trifle more positive in your aspect you would find more success," Vicky pointed out in what sounded like a reasonable tone to Georgia, but only earned her a glare from her sister.

Vicky just turned to Georgia and shrugged. But Georgia only saw it in her peripheral vision. Her gaze had been ensnared. She had finally caught sight of the gentleman she assumed Hilaria had been referring to when she said Lord Crossley was looking particularly fine. She had never seen such a good-looking man before in her life. His tall, athletic build filled out his stylish attire. His full lips would have almost looked feminine if not for the rugged line of his jaw that slanted up toward his bright blue gaze. Much to her disappointment, though, her appreciation of his rugged beauty was somewhat marred by the haughty stare fixed to his face.

Georgia blinked. She really ought not to form an opinion about the man based on a fleeting impression as she caught a glimpse of him from the cramped quarters of a passing carriage. She dismissed all thought of him and applied herself to anticipating her two weeks in the city. It was to be the experience of a lifetime, and she was deeply grateful to her friend for inviting her to tag along as she made her debut.

Of course, poor Vicky wasn't getting a proper debut. Being the third sister and with the first two not yet married, the earl had refused to go to the expense of "properly" launching her as Vicky had lamented. The year before she had been allowed to attend certain events with her older sisters. This year she would be attending along with the older girls, but would not get a ball of her own, nor was she likely to be presented in the queen's drawing room.

Georgia thought it was a shame her friend wasn't going to meet the queen, but she could understand her father's reasoning on the ridiculousness of the court dress. Georgia wondered briefly what the poor queen was thinking to require such elaborate dress of those brought to meet her. The earl was right, of what use would it be to spend so much money on a dress that was to only be worn once? Although, why Vicky couldn't just use the dress that Rosabel had worn when she was presented was beyond Georgia's understanding, but it was really none of her business anyway and she had her own baggage to be concerned about. She once again tore her thoughts away from their fruitless wanderings and brought them back to the task at hand – containing her excitement so as to not draw undue attention to her unsophisticated presence.

When they finally pulled to a stop in front of a large stone house, Georgia assumed they had arrived at the Earl of Sherton's London home. Her swallow felt more like a gulp as she passed her now nervous hands over her skirts, hoping to wipe out the evidence of the many hours of travel. As she watched her hands' nervous movements she absently admired the fabric of the garment. It was one more thing for which to be thankful. As an impoverished girl from the village, Georgia would have nothing that would be appropriate for life in the city. Vicky and her older sisters' generosity in sharing, not only their Season but also their wardrobes, was remarkable. The thought made her want to fling her arms around her friend and squeeze her tight. That, of course, would not do. Not only would it draw Lady Sherton's attention, but it would embarrass Vicky. Georgia resolved to enjoy her two weeks to the ultimate degree and make sure Vicky enjoyed having her there.

With her thoughts thus settled, she was able to step down from the carriage and not quail in front of the imposing structure and the bustle of activity as the ladies were ushered up the stairs and then swallowed by the large open front door. Georgia just hoped she didn't look too much like an owl as her wide eyes tried to absorb every sight they encountered.

Chapter Two

"It would appear the Sherton sisters have arrived for the Season," the Duke of Wexford commented.

The Earl of Crossley couldn't think of an appropriate comment that could be said in public, so he merely sighed in response.

"Are you not delighted by the prospect of three potential mates from one household?" Wexford asked, laughter evident in his tone.

Crossley shot his friend what he hoped was a quelling glare with every intention of maintaining his silence, but when the duke wiggled his eyebrows suggestively, the earl couldn't help pointing out, "I have nothing to fear from those quarters, Wexford, unlike you. The *on dit* is that the oldest one is in search of a coronet. Since there are very few single dukes below the age of fifty, I would be much more concerned about myself, if I were you."

The duke merely shrugged. "While I don't find her single-minded devotion to rank at all attractive, I am not nearly as opposed to the wedded state as you are, so it can remain a source of amusement for me just fine."

Crossley rolled his eyes and returned to his silence.

Wexford chuckled but continued, "The third one seems pleasant. I cannot recall her name at the moment. Not as stunning as the first, but far easier to spend time with. You should take the time to get to know that one."

The earl's glare gained heat, and he lost his silence once more. "I have met the chit. All three of Sherton's daughters have the distinct disadvantage of reminding me of the countess. I have absolutely no desire to extend my acquaintance with them."

This had the desired effect of silencing his companion. Momentarily at least.

"Why do they remind you of the countess?" the duke asked, nothing but curiosity evident in his tone.

Crossley sighed. Ignoring the question, he began walking in the direction they had been heading before they were interrupted by the arrival of Sherton's carriage. "Were we not heading to White's? I dare say I am parched."

A good friend, the duke allowed the earl to avoid the painful subject but did not refrain from another low chuckle before he fell in step with the earl and they made their way to their club.

Crossley couldn't shake his air of dissatisfaction. He hadn't been exaggerating when he said the Sherton girls reminded him of the countess. The duke probably thought he had meant their mother, the Countess Sherton, and he wouldn't have been completely wrong, but Lady Sherton always reminded him of his own countess, and those were thoughts he wanted to keep as far from uppermost as possible.

He had met his late wife through Lady Sherton, and it had turned out to be the ruination of his life. So, no, there was no likelihood of him contemplating marriage with any of the Sherton girls. He had finally managed to scramble his life back together after his wife had destroyed it. He wasn't going to allow Lady Sherton to mess with it again.

~~~

Georgia gazed around the large room.

"I am so sorry that you will have to share with me, George. Mama wants to keep the spare room spare, just in case. I can't tell you what she's expecting might happen, but she wasn't to be persuaded otherwise."

"Please, don't trouble yourself. I should be apologizing to you! I'm used to sharing, but you aren't."

"I think it'll be part of the fun of having you here. It'll be almost like being back in the nursery."

"You want to relive your childhood?" Georgia laughed.

Vicky laughed, too, but then explained herself. "We can giggle and gab over our day before we fall asleep. It's going to be so much better having you here than it was last year," Vicky declared with a grin before it faded a little as another thought struck her. "I only wish you were staying the whole time instead of only two weeks."

"Never mind about that now, Vick. We are going to have such a good time in those two weeks that we won't need any more. Perhaps you'll even be betrothed before I leave, and you'll be just as glad to see the back of me."

This had the desired effect of making her friend burst into laughter. "That would be so perfect. Although, I don't know if Mama would let me get married with Rose and Hil still unattached. But here's to hoping."

Georgia felt her friend's gaze follow her around the room while she spoke. Her curiosity could no longer be contained, and she finally made her way to the wide window. She was delighted to find that it overlooked the street. This discovery prompted her friend into further apologies.
~~~

"I hope it isn't going to bother you being at the front of the house. As the youngest daughter here, we didn't get much choice. But the street isn't too noisy, I promise you."

Georgia dropped the curtain she was holding and ran over to her friend. Finally, she threw her arms around her and gave her a quick squeeze.

"Don't be a goose, Vick. I sleep like a log, so I'm not at all concerned about possible street noise. I have to tell you that I'm actually thrilled that we have a room on the front. I'll be able to watch the street without appearing too ill mannered, I hope. Don't forget, I've never been here before, and my curiosity is nearly killing me." Her gaze searched her friend's face. "Are you terribly worn out from the drive? Or would you be up to at least walking around the block before we change from our travelling attire?"

Vicky had to laugh over her friend's eagerness. "I, at least, had a wall to lean against and managed to nap a little on the drive. I do not know how you can maintain the energy you have. But, yes, I think I can manage a little walk. Mother doesn't have anything planned for the evening so other than our supper, we can spend the time however we'd like."

Georgia clasped her hands in delight. "Then shall we be off?"

With another good-natured chuckle, her friend ushered Georgia back out of the room. Before they left the house, Vicky left word with a footman as to their whereabouts in case her mother did have demands of them, and then they scurried down the front steps.

Georgia schooled her features into what she hoped was an expression of only mild interest, but she allowed her eyes to dance about and take in as much as possible. She was nearly struck dumb by the imposing aspect of the street.

"Do you know everyone who lives on your street?"

"Of course." Vicky laughed. "The *ton* is a very small world, you will soon find. And this isn't a very large street, so it is far from difficult to get to know everyone on it."

Georgia looked at her with a dubious expression. "It might be a small street, but I would say that it would be able to house most of our village, and you still don't know everyone there."

Vicky's fierce blush made Georgia regret her words. "You know why that is," Vicky reminded reproachfully.

"I know. I apologize. I didn't think before I opened my mouth, as usual." Georgia sighed. "I do hope that deplorable trait isn't going to cause us problems while I'm here."

Vicky was quick to get over her ruffled feathers and laughed over the other girl's words. "I doubt it. You're such a kind soul. I doubt you could cause too many problems with your words."

"I hope you're right." Georgia wasn't quite convinced, but she decided to dismiss the thought. "Do you think we could step over into the park while we're here?" They had made their way to end of the street while they talked and were now approaching the famous Hyde Park.

Vicky glanced over her shoulder back toward her father's house. With a shrug, she agreed to her friend's request. "I really doubt Mama will miss us as long as we aren't too long. I promise, we'll come again at the fashionable hour, but for now let us just take a turn around one of these closer trails and then head back. I really ought to be overseeing the unpacking. The maids don't always know what they are about."

Georgia giggled over that. Vicky was a dear but hadn't done any real work in her entire life. Georgia doubted her friend knew what was involved in the packing and care of her wardrobe and thought the maids would be better off without any mistresses ordering them about and making them nervous. But she didn't wish to seem ungrateful, so she merely nodded in agreement with Vicky's pronouncement and stepped briskly down the trail she had indicated.

Happy to be able to breathe deeply after the confines of the carriage, Georgia gazed about at the well-groomed gardens. Georgia's more energetic strides had taken her away from her companion, so she glanced back over her shoulder when she heard a nervous sound coming from Vicky. She hadn't checked her pace, so when she turned her head she felt all the air leave her lungs as she came into sudden contact with a warm wall. Or so it felt. But then the wall grew arms that quickly grasped her and held her back from what turned out to be a well-formed chest encased in what was surely the height of fashion.

Georgia's stunned gaze rose to become ensnared by the blue glare of the one and only Lord Crossley. She couldn't help grinning over his expression. A nervous giggle escaped her, and she felt hot colour flood her cheeks.

"I am terribly sorry, my lord. I failed to watch where I was going. But I must commend you for your quick reflexes on catching me. Thank you for preventing me from injury."

The earl looked incredulous, and Georgia couldn't repress the grin that continued to stretch her cheeks. It was just so obvious the man thought too highly of himself. Of course, he was the most handsome man she had ever laid eyes on as well. Despite the haughty look on his face and the chill of his blue eyes, the brilliance of their colour was enough to capture one's attention. The slight wave in his thick brown hair called to her fingers.

It suddenly dawned on Georgia that she was standing much too close to the handsome nobleman and was grinning at him like a simpleton. She couldn't be sure how much time had passed since she had collided with him but hoped it had been mere fractions of a second. She blinked and took a swift step away from the compelling man. He had yet to say anything, so maybe it hadn't even been a fraction of a second. She realized her thoughts were becoming hysterical, so she finally pulled her gaze away from the earl's face and looked at her friend for guidance.

Vicky arrived at Georgia's side with perfect timing. The much more socially experienced girl bobbed a curtsy and smoothly filled the silence.

"Lord Crossley, what a pleasure to see you again. Might I present to you my friend, Miss Georgia Holton?"

Georgia dipped a curtsy and murmured, "How do you do?"

The earl finally found his tongue. "A pleasure, I'm sure," he almost sneered.

Georgia realized in that moment that the earl certainly thought too highly of himself and seemed to be under the impression that their accidental meeting was not so accidental. She was quite well aware that she was unfamiliar with Town ways and ought to keep her silence on the matter, but she found she wasn't able to.

Despite the fact that he began releasing her hand as quickly as possible, Georgia reacted even faster and it was still in his grasp when she pulled it back and laughed. She looked him straight in his face and strove for a polite tone, but she knew she was being too bold and could only hope Vicky didn't die from the embarrassment.

"Do you really think we would stage such an awkward meeting, my lord?"

He was obviously not expecting such a question. The sneer appeared to be frozen to his face, but his eyes were far less frosty and much more watchful as he waited in silence for her to continue.

Since it didn't appear as though he were going to offer a reply, Georgia continued. "It would seem that you have been accosted in such a manner before and therefore expect such forward behaviour. But, my lord, if I might be so bold as to reason with you for a moment, do you not think we would at least ensure we were in our looks if we were going to arrange such a forward encounter?"

Georgia noticed the earl was no longer sneering, in fact there appeared to be amusement dawning in his gaze, but he still refrained from comment. A quick glance at Vicky showed she had nothing to add and was merely staring at her with a wide, unblinking gaze. Georgia plowed on.

"We have just arrived in Town, we are travel weary, and no doubt quite rumpled. If I were so *gauche* as to wish to stage an encounter with you, my lord, I can assure you, I would ensure that I had at least combed my hair. Now, I cannot comment on the sort of females you normally encounter, but I am quite certain we are not of their ilk."

At this point it finally penetrated Georgia's riled emotions that she was most certainly going too far and had probably offended the handsome man, which would no doubt get back to Lady Sherton's ears and result in her swift dismissal back to the country. She could feel hot colour creeping toward her hairline and was beginning to wish the ground could open and swallow her.

The earl barely blinked as his steady gaze examined her. She felt like a specimen from the traveling circus and lost track of time. It felt as though eons had passed, but surely it was mere seconds? She wondered if she should just turn on her heel and leave. She had run out of words, and it appeared the earl had nothing to say either. If not for the fact that she had no idea how to extricate Vicky from the situation, she would have done just that.

Georgia blinked, sure that she had conjured the sight. The earl was beginning to smile. In fact, his pleasant smile was turning into a toothy grin, and a chuckle sounded from deep in his chest. Crossley looked surprised to hear the sound coming from his own person but didn't suppress it, despite the attention it might draw.

The earl bowed first to Georgia, then Vicky. "Lady Vigilia, might I request the honour of escorting you and your friend to Gunther's?"

Vicky looked flummoxed by the question, and Georgia wished she could jump in and save her, but she finally had a rein on her tongue and managed to remain silent. Apparently, the earl was more comfortable speaking with someone he already knew. Or he didn't think she was capable of polite speech. That thought almost made her snort with derision, but she controlled the urge.

Pale and uncertain, Vicky stammered out a reply. "My lord, that is ever so kind of you to offer, but since we have just arrived in Town, as Georgie mentioned…" She trailed off for a moment in mortification over calling her friend by the diminutive name, but rallied and continued. "That is to say, my lord, that my mother would probably prefer if we return home shortly and change into more suitable attire for going about Town. I'm sure you understand. As Miss Holton said, we merely stepped out of the house for a moment to stretch our, uh…" Here she floundered again, realizing one ought not mention one's legs to an earl. "We just wanted to take a short walk, of course, but surely should be returning home shortly. Perhaps, if you are of a mind to escort us on another occasion, that would be delightful."

"Of course," the earl answered, his suave tone sounding sincere to the point that Georgia almost believed he would call upon them to take them for the offered treat. "In the meantime, might I walk with you for a few moments while you take your restorative stroll?"

Vicky's dubious gaze met Georgia's, and Georgia had to suppress another giggle. She knew Vicky was bewildered how her tirade could have earned the earl's attention, but she did not want to dismiss the man. Even had she wanted to, there was only one answer that could be given.

"It would be our pleasure to have your company, thank you, my lord."

Georgia and Vicky each took one of the earl's elbows, and the trio set off at a steady pace.

"You mentioned you need to be getting home, but how about if we walk over to that copse of trees and then I will escort you back to your house? That will allow us a few minutes to visit together."

"That would be most pleasant," Vicky answered.

Georgia maintained her silence having decided it would be best if she conversed with the man as little as possible, as it was obvious he did not bring out the best in her. However, her resolve was not to last.

"Is this to be your first Season, Miss Holton?" Crossley asked, his tone polite, but his watchful gaze was again lit with amusement as he turned his attention to Georgia.

"Yes, my lord."

"Has your family accompanied you to Town?"

"No, my lord, I will be staying with Lord and Lady Sherton while I am in London."

"How pleasant that will be for the two of you girls."

"It surely will, my lord." She couldn't help accompanying her words with a grin, despite her efforts to maintain a composed demeanour.

"Are you in Town to snare yourself a husband, Miss Holton?"

Georgia wasn't sure what got into Vicky, but all of a sudden her friend launched into speech, saving Georgia from the necessity of coming up with an answer to the uncomfortable question.

"Miss Holton is here merely to keep me company, my lord. She needn't trouble herself with worrying about finding a husband, as she is an heiress."

Georgia flinched when she heard her friend's words and leaned forward to look around the earl to see her more clearly and try to ascertain what she was about. Vicky's laugh sounded a trifle forced to her ears, but Georgia knew it was meant to sound carefree.

"Oh, I suppose we ought to keep that a secret, but you won't tell anyone, will you, my lord? You see, as the younger sister, I found the Season a trifle boring last year, so I prevailed upon Georgia to accompany this time. We plan to just enjoy ourselves and not be bothered with the Marriage Mart, you see, that is why I told you. But I suppose we ought to request your word that you will keep her secret."

"Do you think I am a gossipmonger, my lady?" Crossley's voice sounded equal parts amused and appalled.

"I don't really know you at all, my lord," she answered with a sweet smile that would have made her mother worry if she were there to see it.

Georgia saw and again swallowed her laughter. While she appreciated her friend's efforts to defend her, she couldn't allow her to get into trouble on her behalf. She shook her head at Vicky and quickly stepped into the conversation.

"Why don't we rectify that, my lord? You could tell us a little bit about yourself."

The earl looked surprised by her statement. "What could I possibly tell you that Debrett's hasn't already written about?"

"Lots, I would imagine," Georgia countered with a small laugh. "Why don't we start with something simple like, do you enjoy spending time in London or do you prefer life on your estate?"

Georgia felt his gaze sweep her from head to toe, but she kept her own eyes focused on the scenery of the large park they were strolling through. She felt overwhelmed with the desire to ask him why her question prompted such a reaction from him but daren't pursue the more personal question. Perhaps he was unused to anyone taking an actual interest in him. From what little she knew of High Society it wouldn't surprise her in the least to hear no one actually asked each other for their thoughts.

His tone, when he finally answered, was dry. "Would you believe I can only say both? I do enjoy spending some time in London, but it always ends up feeling like I've stayed too long, and I am relieved to return to my estate." There was a brief silence before he returned the question to the two of them. "What about you? Do you prefer London or the country? I think you, my lady, mentioned that you found London to be a bore?"

"Not at all, my lord, I said the Season was a bore. I quite adore London. It isn't the city's fault that being the third unmarried daughter of an earl is deadly dull."

Crossley laughed over her words but prompted Georgia to answer with a lifted eyebrow.

"This is my first day in London, so I have yet to form an opinion, but I am predisposed to love it from everything I have read and from what Lady Vigilia has told me."

"You have never visited our capital? It seems your education was sorely lacking."

Georgia wasn't sure if his words were meant to be insulting or not, but she decided not to take exception to them. She agreed with him. "That it was, my lord, but it is being rectified now, so we shan't cry over spilt milk."

She couldn't decipher the expression on his face. If she hadn't observed how haughty he had been earlier, she would almost think it was admiration, but that was highly unlikely. *No doubt the man was thinking he had fallen in with a couple of simpletons.* The thought made her want to giggle, but she refrained. It would not do to confirm that opinion.

There was a moment of silence before Georgia thought of a subject she would love to know more about. "Do you sit in the House of Lords, Lord Crossley?"

"I do."

"Is it terribly fascinating?" She recognized the awe in her voice and felt warmth creep up her cheeks again, but she tried to ignore her embarrassment. In her opinion, running the country was a huge responsibility, and she respected those who tried to do it well. Of course, she was well aware that many lords did not make much effort, and that was resulting in growing unrest in some quarters. She had heard murmurs in the village but knew there was much she didn't know.

Chapter Three

Crispin Crossley hoped his fascination was not displayed on his face. The chit hanging onto his left arm seemed to be different from any young woman he had ever encountered before. But he knew he was a terrible judge of character. His countess had fascinated him, too, when he had first made her acquaintance. That meant next to nothing. But he had never heard a young woman show interest in the workings of the government. He felt compelled to tell her about the latest session. But he was interrupted before he even spoke.

"Georgie, don't be silly, his lordship isn't about to tell us any of that. Papa says it's confidential and not for our ears."

The earl smirked. It wasn't true that the workings of the House were confidential, there was actually a visitors' gallery where anyone could stop in and listen if they were so inclined, but it was a good way of getting out of trying to explain to a woman how it all worked. Not that he doubted a woman's ability to understand it, he had just never met a woman who was interested in doing something selfless like trying to make decisions for the benefit of the multitudes.

The young woman's face coloured, and she stammered out an apology. "I had no wish to ask for state secrets, my lord. I didn't realize it would be confidential." He could see that she was frustrated by the thought. Perhaps she had been genuinely curious. He shook his head. It would pass, he reminded himself firmly. Women did not stay interested in such things for long.

Why had he volunteered to spend time with these two chits? He questioned his impulsive decision. He had been intrigued by Miss Holton's reaction to his assumption that their encounter was premeditated. She was nothing like most of the highborn young women he encountered during the Season. Her uniqueness had lured him, but he needed to ignore it and rid himself of his companions as quickly as possible. It was a good thing there were two of them. If he ensured he paid equal attention to them both, it was unlikely he would be raising any sort of expectations with either. Or so he hoped. Heaven knows he had a poor track record when it came to his dealings with the female race.

The silence began to stretch, and Crispin realized he ought to exert himself. Sherton's daughter, the one clutching his right arm, seemed content to walk along at his side. Or so he concluded from the wide smile stretching her face. His friend had been correct, she was a taking little thing and would have probably been a huge success if not for her older sisters. But her grin was probably one of triumph to be seen on his arm, he reminded himself as he turned to glance at the girl on his left. He could see that she no longer looked as confident as she had when she had laughed over his assumptions. She was nibbling her lower lip, a fact that shot an arrow of desire to his core, which he chose to ignore. Besides that, she was casting what appeared to be worried glances at him and trying to catch her friend's eye discretely.

With a silent sigh, the earl gave in to his impulse to set the girl back at ease. He strove for a suitable topic. What does one discuss with a debutante?

"It is a lovely day for a stroll, is it not?" *The weather? That was the best he could come up with?* Crispin realized he had grown socially rusty. He used to be good at this sort of thing.

The Sherton chit merely nodded with an affirmative murmur, but the other miss was prompted into conversation. "Is it unusual to be so fair, my lord? I have heard that the weather in London can be unreliable."

"The temperature is seasonable, I would say, but the rumours you heard were accurate. The weather cannot be counted on. Or should we say rather that the weather can be counted on to be unreliable?"

This nonsensical comment brought a quiet laugh and a small smile to the girl, and Crispin found his chest puffing with pride over his accomplishment. He wanted to roll his eyes but could feel her attention. Strangely, he did not want to hurt her again.

"I must say, though, despite how mild it is, I am rather surprised to see so many people about. And everyone looks so well dressed," she added at the end as she glanced down at her own attire.

Crispin followed her gaze. His wife had been obsessed with fashion and had insisted on educating him on the subject. For that reason, he knew Miss Holton was not dressed in the first stare of fashion, but it was acceptable and not overly travel worn despite the length of time she had no doubt been cooped up in a carriage that day. He could tell her confidence was slipping another notch.

"You look fine," he murmured to her, so as not to be overheard. "If you hold your head up high no one will even question it."

She flashed him a dubious glance but lifted her chin slightly and plastered a tight smile to her lips. He was surprised when she relaxed slightly and asked him a question. He had thought she would maintain her silence as well as her nerves.

"Are most of these people friends of yours, Lord Crossley?"

He glanced around. "Not particularly. Why do you ask?"

He felt her slight shrug. "They all seem to be looking at us. Since I've never met a single soul from London besides the Shertons, and Vicky tells me about all the friends she has, it must be you."

Crispin glanced around again then turned his attention to the girl on his left. "They aren't my friends, but I have a passing acquaintance with most of the people here."

"I'm surprised at the level of curiosity they seem to exhibit about you if they aren't your friends."

"I would advise you to get used to it, my dear girl. The *ton* is nothing if not avidly curious, as you will discover as you go about with your friends."

She wrinkled her nose to display her disbelief, but he just laughed over how much it made her resemble a rabbit. They continued to amble along, making polite conversation. The Sherton girl had finally joined in and added a few thoughts, but it seemed none of them had too much to say. The girls were probably tired from their travels, and he was out of practice in the art of small talk. It was starting to feel as though their walk would never end, even though it had probably not been over long. Crispin was relieved when they left the park behind and were finally on the street.

When they reached the Sherton townhouse the trio stopped at the bottom of the stairs. Lady Vigilia looked up at the house and back at the earl with an expression of anxiety.

"Would you care to stay and greet my mother? We could have tea served."

"No, thank you, my lady. I wouldn't want to put you to the trouble. And since your family has just arrived in Town, your mother may not thank you for bringing guests."

The chit nodded but then had the audacity to laugh. "You *are* the Earl of Crossley, I am most certain she would be happy to entertain you."

Crispin grimaced over her words and asked himself why he had bothered offering to spend time with the two young women. He didn't want to be rude to them, but he had absolutely no intention of raising false hopes in either of them. He was just about to offer a mild set down when Miss Holton stepped into the conversation.

"Vicky, I am most certain his lordship has other things he ought to be doing with his day. He was just being polite to escort us after I bumped into him and interrupted whatever he was about when we encountered him. We really ought to let him take his leave."

Lady Vigilia looked as though she wished to argue but then seemed to accept the wisdom of her friend's words. "Very well. Thank you for your escort, my lord," she said, her tone displaying that her politeness was begrudged.

The other girl didn't say anything at all, just smiled at him and dipped into a curtsy before hurrying up the stairs and into the house. Crispin was surprised to find himself staring at the door after it had been closed, bemused how the inexperienced girl from the country could have so readily dismissed him.

Chapter Four

"What a coup," Vicky crowed as she flopped onto her bed after they had rushed up the stairs to her room and shut the door behind themselves. "Did you see how many people were wondering about what we were doing with Lord Crossley? We shall be the talk of the *ton,* and we have only just arrived." She cast Georgia a reproachful glance. "I still think we should have made him come in for a cup of tea. My sisters would have been beside themselves."

"And your mother would never let us out of her sight again," Georgia countered, her tone dry before adding further reasoning. "Besides, if we had insisted on him remaining for our hospitality, you can be sure he would turn away from us swiftly the next time we encounter him. This way, he will remember that we were not so trialsome, and perhaps he will wish to repeat the experience."

Vicky stared at her with her mouth agape. "You are the most brilliant girl I have ever met. How could you understand such a thing? You have never been to Town before, but you already know how to go on."

Georgia felt a splash of colour on her cheeks and knew her smile was bashful, but all she said was, "People are people, Vicky, whether here or in the village. You might be able to make a man do what you want, but he certainly won't thank you for it."

"Well, you certainly handled the earl expertly. I am sure he will be of assistance to us this Season."

Georgia had to laugh over Vicky's words. "Whatever do you mean? Why would we need assistance? And of what use is the earl to us?"

"I mean to have a much different Season than I did last year. I'm certain being friendly with Lord Crossley can make that happen. I'll happily follow your advice on how to deal with him."

Georgia laughed again. "Not that I have any experience with men, gentlemen in particular. I would think you should be advising me."

Now Vicky laughed. "Very well, then we shall be partners. But you certainly seemed at ease with his lordship for all your inexperience. I think we are going to have a fine time." Vicky paused briefly. "I must say, after all the excitement, I am now ravenously hungry. I do hope the kitchens are preparing something hearty for this evening."

Both girls giggled and carried on discussing their encounter with the earl as well as their plans for the next several days.

"I have to ask you, though, Vick, what made you tell Crossley that I'm an heiress?"

For the first time, Vicky's face creased into discomfort. "I can't really say what came over me, Georgie. I'm dreadfully sorry."

"I'm not looking for your apology. In a certain way, it wasn't a lie. I am inheriting the money from Mr. Byram, since it was from his Will that the Bequest has been set up, but surely you know that isn't the current understanding of being an heiress."

Vicky nodded. "I just launched into speech." She shrugged. "I felt tongue-tied and awkward and felt a moment of jealousy that you had so soundly routed him with your words. I wanted to do the same."

"Jealous? Of me? But we're best friends."

Vicky hung her head. "We are, but we're also almost like sisters. Sometimes sisters can be beasts."

Georgia laughed. "I have a couple of them myself, as you know, so I'm well aware. But it would be strange indeed if word got around that I was an heiress. Your mother wouldn't be pleased, I'm sure."

"Well, the earl did give us his word that he would keep our confidence."

"That he did," Georgia agreed, still uncertain. She then reassured herself with her next words. "To be sure, he probably won't give us a moment's thought anyway, so it isn't something we need to concern ourselves about."

Vicky didn't appear too pleased by this thought, but Georgia quickly distracted her with a change of subject. "What are we to do with the rest of our day?"

"Since we have been traveling all day, we do not have any engagements for this evening, but we are sure to be committed to attend something tomorrow. I will check with Mother as to our agenda, and we can plan what to wear through the day."

"I must thank you again for your generous offer of sharing your gowns with me. I don't think anyone has had such a good friend as you." Georgia was a little ashamed of her circumstances but tried to ignore it.

"Please, say no more. As I have told you already, your being here is thanks enough. Believe me. You are doing me a great service. Everything is so much better when one has a friend by your side. Besides, my sisters and I have more gowns than we know what to do with. It is no hardship whatsoever to share with you. You have already proven your worth this afternoon. Now come along, let us go down to the kitchens and see about some food. I swear I cannot wait until the evening meal."

The two girls traipsed down to the kitchens. Georgia sensed they were making the staff uncomfortable, but they indulged the girls' hunger despite that. Later that evening, Lady Sherton and the four girls had a quiet meal together before retiring for the night. The whirl of activities would begin the next day.

As they prepared for bed, Vicky explained, "Many of the other families have been in Town for at least a week already so in a sense we are a little behind, but Mama hired a modiste to come to Sherton to take our measurements and plan out our new gowns so we wouldn't have to be in residence early. This way we are ready to make the social rounds as soon as we got here. Which is a good thing, since you won't agree to stay any longer than two weeks."

Georgia sighed. Vicky had been harping on this subject since they had made their plans. "I am so grateful for this opportunity and have every intention of enjoying it to the utmost but, as I have told you multiple times, I would hate to overstay your mother's welcome."

"Mama doesn't mind, I promise you."

"Vicky, my heart is warmed by the fact that you want me here with you, but surely you realize that I don't have just myself to think about."

Now Vicky sighed, but hers was much more dramatic. "Your brats will be just fine without you. I really cannot fathom why you give such heed to them."

Georgia chuckled but answered softly. "I'm all they've got, Vick."

Vicky wrinkled her nose and sighed again. "I know, I know, don't worry about me. I realize I am being unfairly selfish for pressing you, but I can already see that having you here is going to be far more enjoyable than without you."

Georgia threw her arms around her friend. "Let us not dwell upon my departure but instead, let us make the most of these fourteen days. It shall be a lark we shall remember always. And you were quite correct. I am ever so glad we needn't spend half my time here making the rounds of all the mantua makers and such. I would find that deadly dull."

"As did I last year, which is why Mama had her brilliant idea of bringing the seamstresses to us. Of course, my sisters were not best pleased. They enjoy the tedious shopping, if you can imagine. Of course, they will, I'm sure, find a way to indulge their fancy. There are still all manner of fripperies to be bought."

Georgia smiled over her friend's comments about her sisters. There were innumerable times that Georgia had wished for older siblings; being the oldest was not the delightful privilege Vicky thought it was. Of course, she might feel differently if she were the daughter of an earl. But as the oldest daughter of the impoverished youngest son of an impoverished baron, she had a far different experience than Vicky's sister, Rosabel. To Georgia's mind, that lovely lady hadn't a care in the world. She knew she ought not make such an assumption, but their circumstances were certainly vastly different.

Not wishing to dwell on the disheartening subject, Georgia quickly changed it. "What do we have planned for tomorrow?"

"The five of us, you, me, my sisters, and Mama, will start making morning calls around noon, and then we are to attend a rout in the evening."

Georgia's giggle brought her explanation to a halt. "What, pray tell, has brought you to such laughter?"

"Why are our visits called morning calls if they are in the afternoon? Whenever you spoke of it in the past, I imagined you were making your rounds in the actual morning."

Vicky laughed over these words but sobered enough to explain. "Surely you realize that in Town the hours are different." After seeing Georgia's hesitant nod Vicky continued. "Since most everyone stays up into the wee hours of the night, breakfast is much later than in the country. So, it would not do to arrive at anyone's door much before noon for fear they might still be breaking their fast or not yet dressed."

"I suppose I never gave it very much thought, but you are quite right, we would not wish to disturb anyone with our visit. It is all so very confusing and yet delightfully exciting. I fear I shan't sleep a wink for all the thrills."

The two girls giggled again as they finished their preparations for bed. With their wide yawns, it was obvious that sleeping wouldn't be much of an issue despite Georgia's words.

Chapter Five

Georgia needn't have worried that she would have trouble with the Town hours. Despite how tired she and Vicky were the night before, they had still ended up talking far too late into the night. That, combined with the long day of travel the day before, led the girls to sleep far later than was usual for the country-bred girls. When Georgia finally came to wakefulness, it was to the quiet shuffling of a maid pulling back the drapes and bustling about the room.

"Sorry miss," the maid whispered when she noticed Georgia's gaze upon her.

"No need to apologize," Georgia whispered back. "From the looks of the sunlight, we have slept half the day away anyway, so we ought to be getting up. Thank you for letting in the light."

The maid bobbed a brief curtsy and left after promising to return with their water. As the door closed behind her, Vicky groaned and covered her head with her pillow.

"Why is it so bright in here? It surely cannot be morning yet. I have barely just closed my eyes."

Georgia laughed. "Don't be daft. We didn't talk that long last night. It couldn't have been even after midnight by the time we fell asleep, and from the looks of the light I would say it is already going on nine o'clock. This is scandalous behaviour in my house. You had best be on death's door if you're going to be staying in your bed so late."

Vicky giggled. "Well, I'll be as fit as a fiddle as soon as I've had my chocolate. Wait until you try it, Georgie. I don't know how they do it, but the kitchens here do a much better job of it than back home. It was the best thing about my Season last year."

Georgia hopped out of the bed. "Well you have me sold. Hurry and get up. I don't want to miss out on this chocolate experience."

Vicky sat up but didn't appear to be in any sort of rush. "Settle down, don't be silly. The maid will bring it to us, there's no need for us to go anywhere."

"Truly? Then why do you have a breakfast room if you don't bother leaving your room to break your fast?"

Vicky stared at her companion without expression for a moment before bursting into giggles. "You are quite correct — it makes no sense except that my father doesn't eat in his room, so there needs to be food served for him somewhere. Also, they will only be bringing us chocolate and toast here. If we wish to have more food, we will adjourn to the breakfast room when we're ready."

"So, the food will just stay there until we see fit to avail ourselves of it?" She wrinkled her nose. "Doesn't it become rather unsavory eventually?"

Vicky wrinkled her nose too but laughed. "No, the servants keep it fresh somehow, no need to worry about that."

Georgia smiled. "I am becoming more and more enamored with the idea of having servants. It would be quite lovely to have someone to prepare and bring me food whenever I have a mind for it."

Vicky stared at her friend once more. "You aren't thinking that you will be doing everything yourself, are you? Even your father has Milly. Surely when you wed you will have someone."

Georgia sighed but tried to keep her smile in place. "I do hope so, but I am trying not to have my heart set on it just in case. But never mind. I shall just enjoy every minute of it while I am here with you," she concluded as the maid returned with the promised water, followed by another servant bearing a tray with toast and mugs of what could only be chocolate. Georgia's mouth began to water at the scent, and she pushed any disquieting thoughts about her future to the back recesses of her mind to be mulled over on her lonely travels back to Sherton. She was determined not to allow her concerns to mar a single moment of her fortnight in London.

The girls took their time getting ready but did eventually make their way to the breakfast room. Georgia silently marvelled over the delicious selections and how lovely they seemed despite having been kept waiting. Soon they were ready for their visits.

As they stood in the foyer of the first house, Georgia thought Vicky had said they were to visit Lady Feversham, but she wasn't perfectly certain. She couldn't help herself from preening ever so slightly as she caught sight of her reflection in the large mirror over the mantel. Georgia had never worn any of Vicky's clothes before. She hadn't thought they were the same size; they certainly looked nothing alike, but the gown suited her remarkably well. In all her days, Georgia was sure she had never worn such a fine garment. Much of her usual wardrobe was made by her own hands, and she was not as skilled as whoever had made this lovely frock. And the pale green suited her to perfection. Georgia had been nearly devastated when Vicky had insisted she would not be able to keep the gown on for the party they were to attend that evening.

"This is most definitely not an evening gown, silly," Vicky had declared.

"But it is beautiful."

"Well, I'm glad you like it, in fact, you can probably keep it, if you'd like, it wasn't even one of my favourites, and it is from last year or perhaps even the year before, so I don't have much need for it."

Georgia smothered her gasp of outrage over her friend's casual attitude to the expense that had no doubt been involved in the acquisition of such an exquisite garment. She must not have been able to keep the dubiousness from her face, though, because Vicky giggled.

"Don't worry about this old gown, George, this is just the first day. I've got even better ones for you for the rest of your time here. And now I'm going to insist that you keep that one after this. It suits you far better than it ever did me or any of my sisters."

Georgia just blinked and nodded, there was very little she could say in reply to such words. Now as she stood admiring her reflection in Lady Feversham's foyer, she marveled anew over her temporary change of circumstances. She wondered if her siblings would even recognize her, were they to see her at a glance. Not that she usually looked like a dowd, she did her best to always be presentable. But she had never before had the assistance of a lady's maid and today she was pretty much all the crack, if she did say so herself. Her reflection grinned back at her, and Georgia made every effort to compose her features before their hostess found her admiring herself. She tore her gaze away from the unfamiliar sight of herself looking to be in the height of fashion and looked around the beautiful foyer instead.

It was even grander than the foyer at Sherton House or the Sherton's townhouse, the only two noble houses she had ever visited. But those two houses were large and beautiful. Georgia would never have thought anywhere could be more spectacular. The marble floors gleamed and the sunlight streaming through the large stained glass window above the door cast colourful twinkles throughout the large space. Georgia made every effort not to look like someone fresh from the country as she looked around. She doubted that she had succeeded. They were led into a spacious receiving room that was even more beautiful than the foyer, much to Georgia's delight.

Lady Feversham, Georgia had remembered the name accurately after all, was a pleasant but seemingly bird-witted lady of middle age. She put Georgia in mind of a little brown hen as she fluttered around the room greeting all her visitors. There were perhaps too many of them in their group. Five women arriving all at once might be a bit much for the most stalwart of hostesses, she mused. But Lady Feversham rallied and settled her plumage as they all were seated, and Georgia was introduced as the family friend that she was.

Their hostess was polite but didn't exude an excessive interest in Georgia, so she sat back and enjoyed watching the byplay of the social interaction. While she, of course, visited the various inhabitants of their small village, she had never found herself in such a sumptuous situation. Even though Vicky's home, Sherton House, was wonderful, it was familiar, and they rarely stood on ceremony anyway. Too, there was the fact that Georgia didn't know any of the people under discussion. But it mattered not. It was highly diverting to listen to the ladies' conversation, and she felt no need to interject.

Georgia found it interesting to watch Rosabel and Hilaria acting as young ladies rather than older sisters as well. Georgia didn't think Hilaria was capable of such pleasant interaction. She was the least aptly named of the Sherton sisters. Lord Sherton enjoyed his Latin and had insisted that his newly born second child was going to be a cheerful sort. He was sadly mistaken, but it was a pretty name nonetheless.

Musing on the two older girls, Georgia reflected on the relationship she had previously developed with them. Despite their poverty, because Georgia was wellborn, she had been allowed to run around Sherton House with Vicky since they were little girls. They had been born within days of one another and had been fast friends since they had been toddling. Rosabel and Hilaria had always taken themselves far more seriously than Vigilia ever did, so they had looked down their noses at the younger girls, at times tolerating their presence better than at others. So, it was strange for Georgia to see them being polite and proper as they chatted with their hostess.

It was fascinating, really. But Georgia supposed even she herself was different depending on the role she played – nursemaid to her ailing father, mother to her young brothers and sisters, friend to the Sherton girls, steward of her father's small home. She had never really looked at the Shertons as ladies, and it gave her a slight pang to recognize that she would soon be far out of their league. Georgia pushed the unwelcome thought away and determined once again to enjoy every last minute of these two weeks.

The allotted fifteen minutes passed in what felt like the blink of an eye and before she knew it, Georgia was following the others back into the foyer and out onto the street. The process was repeated two more times before they returned to the Sherton's townhouse to prepare for their evening.

"The staff will have laid a light luncheon for us in the breakfast room, girls, and you ought to eat something before you dress for the rout. While Lady Shaftesbury is a gracious hostess and generous to a fault, her cook is not the best, so you better not be too hungry when it comes time for supper," Lady Sherton admonished as they removed their spencers and handed their bonnets to the footmen. "Not that young ladies should ever appear too hungry," she concluded as an aside.

Georgia prevented her eyes from rolling at this direction and meekly followed the others to the breakfast room. As she filled her plate, she realized that making three calls in an afternoon worked up an appetite. She had thought she would never be hungry while she was lazing about in London, but the life of a lady of leisure took more effort than she had anticipated.

All the women were preoccupied with thoughts of the evening to come, so conversation was desultory as they made quick work of the meal. Before long Georgia and Vicky were back in their room and Vicky was called upon to once again assure her companion that a walking gown would not do for the evening.

"But Vick it's just so beautiful. Surely it would be acceptable," she almost pleaded.

"You haven't even looked at the gown you are to wear this evening, so how can you be sure it's not far better than this one?" Vicky reasoned with a laugh.

"It isn't possible to be more beautiful," Georgia insisted until she turned to the maid and gasped with delight. "Oh my stars, I stand corrected," she breathed as she admired the gown the servant was holding for her to view.

The intricate embroidery over the white netting was in Georgia's favourite shade of green. The same green could be seen in the trim along the hem. Georgia was delighted to see that while the neck was round, it wasn't dreadfully low. She would have no reason to be uncomfortable. The short sleeves were puckered into a delightful puff. Georgia knew she would be admiring herself in any mirror she might encounter that evening. She wouldn't be able to get over how very lovely the gown was. It was doubtful she would ever see such a sight again.

Georgia was embarrassed to be so in awe as the maids scurried around helping her and Vicky prepare. She had thought herself inured to the Shertons' status, both social and financial, but she was feeling decidedly subdued as it was brought home to her mind just how completely out of her usual depth she was. And it all seemed so commonplace to Vicky, Georgia marvelled. She just hoped she didn't embarrass her friend and the Sherton family during her two weeks there with her backward, provincial ways.

When she realized the direction of her thoughts, she forced some steel back into her spine. Just because the Shertons were better off than she was didn't make them better than her. And she wasn't such a bumpkin as all that. Before her own dear mama had died, she had taught her everything she needed to know to be a part of the *ton*. Just because Georgia had never had much opportunity to use that education didn't mean she was going to shame anyone. In fact, Georgia thought fiercely, she was a Holton, and while they had fallen on hard times, that didn't mean it was anything to be sneered at.

With those bracing thoughts, Georgia allowed her eyes to finally stray to the mirror. She had been steadfastly avoiding eye contact with herself or the maid as she fussed with her hair. Now she took in the sight of the servant's handiwork and it was all she could do to restrain an ill-bred whistle from leaving her lips.

"You have outdone yourself, Sally. Thank you so very much!"

Vicky came up behind her. "Isn't she a wizard with hair? You are sure to turn some heads tonight," the loyal friend admired.

Georgia watched the colour rising in her cheeks over her friend's compliment but forbore to comment. Her gaze instead examined Vicky. "You clean up fairly well yourself," she teased. "That colour particularly complements you. Although darker would probably suit you even better. Tell me again why we are restricted to pastel and light colours only."

Vicky merely shrugged. "I think it's just the fashion. And it clearly identifies who the debutants are in case anyone was wondering." Both girls chuckled over her words. Georgia's mirth was quickly muffled as the maid carefully slid her gown over her artfully arranged hairstyle.

"You look just like a picture in the fashion plates, Miss," Sally admired.

"It's all due to your hard work, thank you, Sally."

"Now come along, it wouldn't do for us to be dallying," Vicky admonished as she herded her friend out of the room.

The two girls made their way to the foyer. They were the first to arrive but they were soon joined by Vicky's sisters and mother. After Lady Sherton inspected them each carefully, making Georgia feel like a specimen from the circus once more, she declared them all set, and the five of them made their way out to the waiting carriage. Once again, Georgia found herself needing to stem her mounting excitement.

Chapter Six

Crispin was standing across the room when the Shertons and their companion were announced. He had never been one to admire such young ladies, but he couldn't help feeling his heart skip a beat when his gaze encountered his new acquaintance, Miss Georgia Holton. The chit was ravishing this night.

"Who is the lovely creature in company with the Shertons?" his friend Charles Layton drawled by his side. "She seems to have snagged your attention quite neatly."

Maybe calling the man his friend was being a little too generous, Cris thought as he struggled to formulate a suitable reply. "Just another heiress here to make her mark on Society," he replied, forcing boredom into his tone even as he remembered that the young ladies had sworn him to secrecy. "Actually, my good fellow, I may have misspoken. I don't rightly know much about the chit, just met her in the park recently. Aren't all the debutants heiresses? I may have confused her with another."

Charles gazed at his companion with speculation glowing in his eyes. "You have no need for any extra blunt, so I have no idea why you'd be trying to hide an heiress from me. Why would you bother setting your sights on an heiress anyway?"

Crispin struggled to keep his growl contained. "I'm not setting my sights on anyone, Layton. Don't go starting any such hideous rumours."

Charles' chuckle was almost friendly. "Pay me no mind, my lord. Your secret is safe with me."

The earl doubted that, but there was nothing else he could do to salvage his mistake. Shrugging, he turned away from both the sight of the Sherton ladies and the pest by his side. Hailing another passing gentleman, his forced disinterest soon became reality as he forgot about the newest maiden in Town and became absorbed in the political discussion he was involved with. It wasn't until halfway through the evening that he would recall the brief exchange and wish Lord Charles Layton to perdition for not the first time.

Georgia made every effort to keep her amazement under control. Vicky had assured her the evening would not be a squeeze. She wondered how many more people would need to be jammed into one set of rooms in order for the gathering to gain that description. As it was, it felt to Georgia as though the room were filled wall to wall with people. She said as much to Vicky.

"Oh no, Georgie. Don't you see that we can easily walk around and converse reasonably well with people? At a gathering that would be termed a crush, you would barely be able to hear me and it would be challenging to navigate the room."

Georgia examined her friend's face to verify if she were indeed telling her the whole truth, at least from her own perspective. Vicky's face and posture exuded seriousness. Georgia had to believe her. She was not teasing, and Vicky was far more experienced about *ton* ways than Georgia so she ought not doubt her friend's word. But it was difficult to believe that anyone would enjoy attending such a crowded gathering. With a mental shrug, she added to the list of odd things she had taken note of about highborn Society and decided it mattered little. She was following Vicky's lead during her visit and would have no say over which events they were to attend no matter how crowded they might be predicted to be. She would merely thank her blessings that her first official event was no more crowded than it was.

Glancing around, she was happy to see that she recognized a few faces. They had met with a few of those present when they had been making calls earlier that day. And through the crowd, into the next room, she was almost certain she had glimpsed the back of Lord Crossley's head. Not that she really knew what the back of his head looked like, but it had struck her as familiar, and a small frisson of recognition went through her. She shook her head. It would certainly not do for her to become fixated on the haughty earl. Nothing but heartbreak was at the end of that particular path. She pushed the man from her thoughts and renewed her determination to enjoy the evening.

"Is that not the most fascinating piece of sculpture you've ever seen?"

Georgia was startled from her perusal of said sculpture by the sound of a deep voice just behind her. She turned with a small smile to acknowledge the man's words. They had not been introduced, and she was unsure if she should engage in conversation with him, but she couldn't bear to be rude. Or rather, it seemed rude to her not to acknowledge his words. Perhaps she was out of line. Her indecision must have been written on her face.

"Forgive me, my lady, it was evident that we were both admiring the piece. But you are right, we have not yet been introduced. I will find someone to do the honours and return to you."

Georgia watched in fascination as the man disappeared into the crowd as quickly as he had appeared. She glanced back toward Vicky, who had been caught up in a conversation with another young lady and hadn't witnessed the strange exchange. Georgia acknowledged to herself that it couldn't even be rightly called an exchange, as she hadn't even spoken to the man. She shook her head. What a strange evening.

"Are you enjoying yourself?" Vicky asked, keeping her tone low in the crowded room so Georgia had to strain to hear her.

She smiled at her friend's attempt at discretion.

"I am, indeed. I just had a strange encounter, though, with a gentleman who remarked upon the sculpture I was admiring. But then he disappeared into the crowd."

"Oh, who was it?" Vicky turned to look.

"I have absolutely no idea. We have not been introduced, and I've never seen him before. You do remember this is my first full day in London."

Vicky smiled at Georgia's dry tone.

They made their way into another room where music was being played and a few couples were making up a country dance. Georgia grinned. Her feet would be delighted to do some dancing.

"Good evening, Lady Vigilia, how pleasant to see you here this evening." They were startled by a deep voice behind them, and both girls turned to see who was addressing them.

"Oh, good evening, Lord Layton. How do you do?" Vicky replied politely, but Georgia noticed the reserve hidden in her tone.

"I am well, thank you. It seems you have a new friend with you."

Vicky's laugh was light and brief. "This is not a new friend. She is, in fact, my oldest friend, Miss Georgia Holton."

Turning to Georgia, she finished the introductions. "Georgia, might I present the viscount, Lord Charles Layton?"

Georgia dipped into an appropriate curtsy nearly overwhelmed with curiosity about the gentleman, although everything in her was alert to be on guard over Vicky's obvious hesitance. Realising it would only be obvious to her because of their long acquaintance, Georgia admired her friend's social skills.

She had yet to even say a greeting to the man when he quickly launched into speech. "Might I have the pleasure of your hand when the next set forms?"

Her gaze flew to Vicky's. She knew her friend was on guard about this man but had no idea why. He seemed well spoken, socially acceptable, even handsome. And Vicky had said he was a viscount. It really mattered very little why Vicky was guarded about the man. There was nothing Georgia could say except, "It would be a pleasure, my lord, thank you."

While they waited, they would have to make conversation. Vicky didn't seem to have much to say, and Georgia was just thinking that she would have to step into the silence when the viscount spoke up.

"Where do you come from, Miss Holton?"

"Not too far from the Shertons," she answered briefly, without supplying any details.

"Ah, yes, she did say you are her oldest friend. How nice." His tone left Georgia feeling as though she ought to contribute something more.

"Are you very familiar with Wiltshire, my lord?"

"Not overly. In fact, I've never visited Pembroke. But it's not too terribly far from Bath, is it? I've been there, of course."

"Of course," she murmured, feeling laughter wanting to bubble up her throat and hoping fervently her amusement did not display itself upon her features. Vicky would either kill her or die of mortification if she were to insult a viscount by laughing at him. She didn't bother commenting on how far she lived from Bath. It wasn't overly far if she understood correctly, but she didn't want to admit to this man that she had never been there.

She was relieved when the musicians drew the current dance to a close and announced the next one. Her relief was deepened to hear it was a cotillion, but it did not appear there would be too many couples so it needn't last forever. With all the changes, she wouldn't have to engage in much conversation with the viscount.

But she needed to say something. "You didn't mention where you are from, my lord. I am sure most everyone here knows who you are and where you live, but since I'm new to Town, I must confess my ignorance."

The viscount grinned at her. Georgia realized if she had read up on her Debrett's or memorized it, as Lady Sherton had advised, she would not have needed to ask this. She had thought the advice was useless when she had heard it, but now she was facing the reality that Lady Sherton knew what she was talking about. With an inward sigh, she looked at the viscount expectantly, hoping he would not remark upon her mistake.

"That is quite all right, my dear," he began, his tone slightly condescending. "My father is the Marquis of Swinton. His primary seat is in Norfolk."

"Oh, it must be lovely there," she remarked.

He grinned again. *He probably thinks I'm angling for an invitation,* Georgia thought before realizing with dawning horror, *Or he thinks I'm anticipating the potential of making it my home one day.* Her stomach turned as she realized how ridiculous this Marriage Mart truly was. She immediately questioned the wisdom of accompanying her friend even for only two weeks.

She had to brazen her way through the awkward moment and waited for him to speak next. Blessedly the steps separated them for a moment and she was able to pretend she had no such thoughts and merely looked at the viscount expectantly.

"My father is certainly proud of the place," was his only comment.

There was more silence between them. It wasn't truly awkward as the steps of the dance made conversation, not impossible, but certainly unnecessary. Georgia began to enjoy herself once more. She should not have let down her guard. Once more, they came together.

"I have heard you are an heiress, Miss Holton. Was your father in trade?"

Georgia nearly stepped on his foot, she was so surprised. She wondered what was the best way to handle the gentleman. She decided on the truth.

"I find you are being impertinent, my lord. I am not an heiress."

"Ah, he did say he wasn't supposed to say anything. Why the secrecy?"

"Who said this to you?"

Now, the viscount turned sly. "If you are going to keep secrets, then I think so will I."

Georgia felt her colour ebbing and then flooding back as she realized Lord Crossley must have been gossiping about her. She had to contain her fury. It would not do to kick the viscount in the shins and stomp off to find the earl. Instead, she offered her dance partner the sincerest smile she could muster and changed the subject.

"Do you come to London for the Season every year, my lord?"

"Of course, what else is there to do?"

Georgia almost rolled her eyes as she thought of the myriad other things they could be doing. "Are you involved in Parliament then?"

"No, the marquis doesn't trust me with any of the seats." His words confirmed to Georgia just how very indolent the viscount was. Even his father didn't trust him to be able to do the work.

"That is unfortunate," she murmured.

"Not really. I am just as happy to leave all that to others."

Georgia knew her smile was wan but could muster no enthusiasm for continuing the conversation. She perked up when she heard the music coming to a conclusion.

When the viscount returned her to Vicky's side, Georgia dipped into another curtsy. "Thank you, my lord." She didn't elaborate. She didn't have much good to say about the experience. Vicky saved either of them from having to speak further.

"We really ought to be checking in with my mother, Georgia."

"Of course," Georgia answered with a smile.

"It was a pleasure to make your acquaintance, Miss Holton. Might I call upon you one day this week?"

Georgia blinked but quickly recovered. "I cannot say for certain which days we shall be at home, my lord, as we have just arrived in Town. But we are sure to run into you somewhere throughout the week, I am sure."

It would seem the lazy viscount wasn't stupid and did have a sense of humour to redeem him. He chuckled. "Very well, Miss, I accept that I am being dismissed. I will allow it for now. You can be sure you will be seeing me." With a bow that encompassed them both, he departed.

When their gazes met, both girls had to bite their lips to keep from bursting into laughter.

"That was an experience to write home about," Georgia commented. "The daft man asked me about being an heiress. I could hardly credit it, but it would seem the earl has been telling tales."

"No!" Vicky exclaimed. "I did not think he would be so churlish."

Georgia giggled. "Which one? The viscount or the earl?"

"Both, really," Vicky replied with a grin. "I didn't think Layton would press you on such a subject, nor did I think Crossley would reveal what we told him was a confidence."

Georgia shrugged. "It would seem men are just as subject to gossip as the old women in the village."

Vicky giggled. "You are right about that. But so my words aren't a lie, let's go find the countess and see if my sisters are intent on remaining here much longer."

After they spoke briefly with Lady Sherton and found out that Rosabel was having too good a time to consider leaving any time soon, the girls wandered to another room.

"Your mother seems quite intent on arranging a match for Rosabel," Georgia commented.

"Well, it *is* her third season, and there are five of us girls," Vicky reminded her. "It would seem a daunting task to the most stalwart, I am sure."

Georgia giggled. "At least Bel is beautiful. She must have received many offers."

"Myriads if you could believe her. But I am sure she has received many. And in all honesty, I cannot blame her for being choosy. It is a momentous decision. It is the rest of her life she has to decide about."

Georgia felt a shudder slither down her back at the thought of the seriousness hidden by the seemingly joyous events of the Season. "Does it worry you?"

Vicky shrugged. "I have time. And I have the advantage of being able to watch my sisters make their choices first." She turned her searching gaze upon Georgia. "What about you? It seems to me, you are in the same boat. Even worse, now that I think on it. You will need to marry as well as possible, and your choices are more limited. Unless you find someone while you're here." Vicky seemed to warm to her subject. "You truly ought to try, Georgie. Wouldn't it be far better to marry a member of the *ton*? There would be a much better chance of us seeing each other in the future. And wouldn't you be in a better position to help your brothers and sisters if you could become a peeress?"

"Really, Vicky, have you taken leave of your senses? Which peer is going to marry a country bumpkin with a ten-pound dowry and three or four hungry siblings in tow, depending if Gregory is around or not? I'm not that good looking, and I might even be considered a bluestocking."

Ever loyal, Vicky insisted, "You are beautiful, especially now that you have the assistance of proper hairstyling. I must say I have never seen you look better than you do tonight. If Rosabel was not so self centered, I would think she would be green with envy of your looks this evening, but I dare say she didn't even take notice. And I would be absolutely mortified except that I love you dearly."

Georgia giggled along with her friend but then sobered as Vicky continued. "And while I know you are a bluestocking, you are quite adept at hiding it, so I do not think it would necessarily hold back any of the gentlemen. Only the fortune hunters would truly care about a lack of funds on your part. Or those seeking a dynastic marriage for some reason. But you are eligible enough, sociably speaking. I am absolutely certain you could find any number of eligible gentlemen who would be honoured to take you as their bride. Since you don't have your heart set on anyone back home, I don't see why you wouldn't consider it."

"But Vicky," Georgia almost pleaded as she tried to get her friend to see reason. "Don't you see? I would feel at a disadvantage if I come to a marriage so lopsided. I was not raised to it like you were. I've been raised to bring my skills to a marriage. And my ten pounds is supposed to be an asset, not the punchline to a joke."

Vicky refused to give in. "You, Georgia Holton, would be the asset you would bring to any marriage. Any man, whatever his circumstances, would be lucky to have you."

Georgia felt tears well in her eyes from her friend's kindness. "You are the best friend ever, Vicky, and I thank you for your kindness, but I still don't think I want to find myself a husband amongst the *ton*."

Vicky sighed and relented. "Very well, I shan't press you further now, but I reserve the right to bring this up for discussion at another time."

There wasn't much else Georgia could do but grin over her friend's words. Then she felt a shiver of awareness slither deliciously up her spine. She turned her head and wasn't overly surprised to see the earl, Lord Crossley, approaching.

Chapter Seven

Georgia turned back to face Vicky, wondering how to correctly handle the situation. She wanted to ring a peal over the wretched man but did not want to cause an ill-bred scene to embarrass the Shertons. She wasn't even sure if she could rely on Vicky to help her out of the awkward situation, as her eyes were brimming over with mirth.

"Good evening, Lady Vigilia and Miss Holton. What a pleasure to see you here."

"My lord," Georgia acknowledged with a barely perceptible curtsy and her tone devoid of warmth while avoiding eye contact. Vicky maintained perfectly appropriate behaviour, dipping low and murmuring, "How do you do?"

"Miss Holton, might I have the pleasure of your company when supper is served?"

"Will you gossip about it like a maiden aunt if I refuse?" she countered, ice dripping from her voice.

"I beg your pardon?"

Georgia would have grinned over his shock if she were not too livid to appreciate the humour. It was doubtful the wretch had ever been denied in his life. He probably thought he misheard, she surmised.

"I would rather starve than go in to supper with you," she stated in a low but clear voice. Georgia was well aware it was socially unacceptable to refuse such an invitation, that calling it an invitation was just being polite, but she couldn't find it within herself to care.

The earl gazed at her blankly for a moment before bursting into laughter. "You are most definitely an original, Miss Holton." When he realized that she wasn't even slightly joking, he sobered. "Might I ask what has led you to take me in such dislike that you cannot even share a meal with me?"

"I had the dubious pleasure of making the acquaintance of Lord Layton," she stated, still not making eye contact with him and making every effort to not draw attention to her anger. But the effort was making her feel as though her hair were going to melt.

"Ah, I see." The earl took a deep breath. "Might I have a few minutes of your time over supper to stammer out my apology?"

"If you think to earn your way back into my good graces by being cute, you can think again, my lord, as I am not nearly that fickle." Her anger was certainly not diminishing, as she saw amusement in his face. "Laughing at me isn't going to help very much either," she added, her dry tone adding to the laughter in his eyes.

Vicky, though, was not finding the situation amusing. She pinched Georgia's arm, making her jump and stifle a squeak. "We would be delighted to dine with you this evening, my lord, thank you so much for your kind invitation," she said, overriding Georgia's outrage and offering the earl a sweet, if fake, smile.

The pain in her arm where Vicky's sharp fingers had surely left a dent brought Georgia to her senses. She could not give an earl the cut direct, nor insult him by refusing him in such a way. She swallowed the sour taste of impotent rage and offered him an insincere smile of her own. Georgia refused to lie and could not say it would be a pleasure. So, she kept her mouth shut. She knew she was flushed and wished she had a fan to cool her red face. *Why would he want to spend any time with us anyway*, she wondered, as she exerted an effort not to cross her arms and stamp her foot. She knew she would regret it later if she made a scene now, but part of her wanted to kick the man in the shins and walk away.

Taking another quick peek at him, she saw that his amusement had not faded so she averted her eyes, took a deep breath, and counted to ten. It didn't help all that much except that making the effort amused her. It reminded her of how many times she had to count to ten not to lose her temper with her siblings, and thinking of them helped her regain control over her roiling emotions. It crossed her mind to wonder why she had been less angry with Drew when he cut off Marianne's braids than she was with the earl at this moment. Perhaps she had higher expectations of adults. But she really didn't expect very much from a member of the *ton*. Her anger was excessive. She should not be disappointed in him. It is not as though they had a relationship that was now marred by his breach of her trust.

Georgia took another deep breath. She was being insufferable. Just because the earl was being a cad didn't mean she needed to stoop to his level. She lifted her chin, braced her shoulders, and looked him in the eye without flinching. She would have sworn she saw admiration in his gaze but that was unlikely. It was much more likely that she was losing her mind, she thought with a wry twist of her lips.

"I wonder what our hostess is serving," she mused in a steady, calm voice, but heard a snort coming from the direction of the earl. She did not turn to verify her assumption, merely continued to walk between him and Vicky in the direction of the supper room.

Georgia barely took note of what was on her plate. It required every ounce of her concentration to maintain the veneer of politeness needed to smile and nod in all the correct places as Vicky did her valiant best to conduct a conversation with the earl. Georgia felt Lord Crossley's puzzled gaze resting on her from time to time, but she managed to avoid making eye contact. It was all she could do to swallow the no doubt delectable food that only tasted of sawdust in her mouth. Finally, she couldn't put another bite into her mouth. She placed her cutlery on her plate, and an attentive footman quickly stepped forward to take it away.

"Now that you've been fed, would you be so kind as to tell me what exactly happened with Lord Layton to give you a disgust of me?" Crossley asked, his deep voice sending a thrill through her, despite her anger with him.

Incredulous, Georgia stared at him as though he were an imbecile, which she seriously thought he might be. *How does the man manage to maintain his fortune and his position in Society if he is so dull-witted?*

"You told him I'm an heiress," she finally managed to spit out without yelling.

"Did you not tell me yourself that you are an heiress?" he countered, although Georgia noticed that he was beginning to look contrite.

"We also asked you to keep it a secret."

Now the earl was beginning to look shamefaced. "I didn't mean to tell him. It just slipped out. And when I tried to take it back, he became very sly with me as though I was trying to get one over on him." There was a moment of silence while the three exchanged glances. "Is it really so bad if people know you're an heiress?"

Finally, Georgia couldn't take it anymore and she burst into laughter. "The problem is, my lord, that I am not really an heiress. I am a well-born girl of no means. In our town, there is a bequest for all the impoverished girls to receive a small dowry. A potentially life-changing inheritance for me. Not so much for a member of the *ton*."

"But will it really matter if people think you are an heiress?" He clearly didn't understand.

Georgia sighed. "From a certain perspective, probably not. In the grand scheme of things, I am just a girl from the country here to enjoy the city for a few days with my friend. But it has the potential to court controversy that could make my short visit uncomfortable and embarrass my hosts."

"I do offer you my sincerest apologize, my dear Miss Holton. I truly wish I could take my words back, but there doesn't appear to be much that can be done about it."

"You are quite correct, there is nothing that can be done at this point. I shall do my best not to hold a grudge." She offered him a wan smile. After glancing at Vicky to see that she had nothing more to add and was ready to leave, Georgia got to her feet. "No doubt, we will see you again sometime." She dipped into a more respectful curtsy than her last one and departed from him without a backwards glance.

"You were magnificent, Georgie," Vicky commented. "I could barely credit it when you nearly gave him the cut direct. I hope you aren't furious with me for forcing you to spend the supper with him. I just couldn't bear it if we caused a scene."

"Of course not, my dear friend. You were perfectly correct. It would not have done to make a public spectacle of ourselves. Thank you for forcing me to come to my senses. Hopefully it was all a tempest in a teacup for nothing and Lord Layton will keep his thoughts to himself and it will all turn out to be a nonissue." The two girls exchanged a glance. "That's not too likely, is it?" She sighed. "Ah well. I have had worse things said about me than that I'm an heiress. Let's not allow it to trouble us further. We shall deal with matters as they arise." After bracing her shoulders, she put her arm through Vicky's.

"Now, come along. I overheard a gentleman say someone is singing in the library. I would like to see that for myself."

With that, the two girls resolved to enjoy the rest of their night.

Chapter Eight

"You seem terribly pensive this evening, Crossley. What is ailing you, my friend?"

The earl barely acknowledged the duke's words, keeping his eyes focused on the amber liquid in the glass in front of him, but he did allow the corner of his mouth to tip up in some semblance of a crooked smile.

Wexford wasn't going to leave it there. He snapped his fingers in front of his friend's face. "Hello, Crossley, hello. What is the matter with you tonight? You are nowhere near as amusing as usual. Do you not know that is why we keep you around? You are no longer holding up your end of the bargain."

This finally had the desired effect. Crispin shook off his pensive mood. Laughter danced in his eyes as he finally focused his gaze on the duke's face.

"I am not the amusing one, your grace, and well you know it."

"Ah, perhaps I was mistaken," the duke agreed with a grin. "Now tell me, what is troubling you?"

"Naught is troubling me, Duke. I have no idea what you are talking about." Crispin tried to evade his friend's questions.

"Do not think you can gammon me. You have not said more than three words since you got here. And don't bother trying to tell me that you're tired because I don't think the clock has even struck midnight. The debutantes are probably still dancing vigorously. You cannot be tired."

Crispin again offered the duke a lopsided smile. This time he added a shrug for good measure. "I must just not have much to say this evening."

"Is it Christopher? Is there something wrong with the boy?"

This wasn't the best topic to question. The smile was swiftly wiped from the earl's face to be replaced with another scowl. "As far as I know, the boy is right as rain." Crossley countered a glare from the duke. "Do not get all ducal with me, your grace. I've known you since you were still in leading strings and had no thought to being the heir. You might be able to glare others into submission, but you'll catch cold trying that with me."

The duke's glare melted into a soft smile. "Well then, if we have truly been friends for that long then you surely shouldn't be keeping anything from me. Now tell me. What has you in the doldrums? It must be a woman. I haven't seen you like this before, but the only time it has come close it is always a woman."

Crispin tossed back the last of the liquid in his glass. "I swear to you, Wexford, I am perfectly fine." He paused briefly and tried to hold up under the expectant stare of his childhood friend. Finally, with a soft sigh and a stifled epithet he nodded. "If you must know, I do have something on my mind." Again, the duke said nothing, only raising his eyebrows even further in inquiry. The earl's sigh was louder this time. "I broke my word today."

The duke blinked in surprise. He had never known the earl to ever break his word. It was a matter of honour to most gentlemen, but Crossley was particularly particular about keeping his word.

"That is surprising." The duke paused. "Did you have a good reason for doing so?"

"Not really."

The silence stretched while the duke waited him out. He refilled each of their glasses from the decanter that the waiter had left conveniently by his elbow. The earl took a healthy draft. It must have finally loosened his tongue.

"It was that imbecile Layton that made me do it."

The duke again used his eyebrow to good effect.

Crispin felt the colour rising in his cheeks. "I know, any man of sense should not be put out by an imbecile such as Layton, but he happened to be standing by me when the Shertons and their friend arrived. I do not know what Layton thought he saw on my face, but he began to speak about Miss Holton in such a way that I felt the need to punch his face. Instead, without thought, I said something about the young woman that it was not my place to say. Now she is furious with me. Rightly so, of course, but I do not know how to make amends. I have never found myself in this strange position before."

The earl would have laughed if he were not in such a disturbed mood. Wexford's jaw appeared to have become unhinged for a moment before he regained his usual equanimity and his eyebrow returned to its elevated position. And then he chuckled. "I knew it had to be about a woman." His tone bordered on gleeful.

Crispin stared at the duke, incredulous. "Out of everything I said, that's what you have picked up on?"

The duke shrugged. "You didn't actually say all that much. I am shocked that you allowed Layton to get the better of you, and it goaded you into doing something so uncharacteristic as to break your word. But I am delighted that it involves a woman. If you could be goaded into doing anything because of a woman it gives me hope for you, Cross. You need to find joy in your life."

Crispin's stare had begun to morph into a glare, but the duke's last words surprised a chuckle out of him. "You are beginning to sound like my mother, Duke."

"I shan't take that as an insult — your mother was a lovely woman."

"But she was a woman. You are not. You ought not to be saying such things as observing that I need joy in my life. It sounds quite unmanly."

The duke's chuckle accompanied his shrug. "I am man enough to say such a thing. And it is true. You have lived in a dark cloud for too many years."

Both men took another healthy sip from their glasses.

"Now tell me, just how angry is the young woman? Perhaps I can help you figure out how to get back into her good graces."

"I didn't say I want to be in her good graces," Crispin growled.

"You were plenty melancholy about it. I would say you do," the duke pointed out reasonably.

"I was feeling melancholy, as you say, because I dishonoured myself as a gentleman by breaking my word. I really couldn't care less about Miss Holton's feelings."

"That doesn't sound terribly honourable to me, Cross," Wexford observed, although he seemed to be having trouble keeping a grin off his face. "A gentleman should always have a care for a lady's feelings."

Cris felt the heat rising in his cheeks once more. Part of him wanted to cross his arms, stamp his foot, and mutter that Miss Holton hadn't had a care for his feelings. Instead, he had to agree with the duke. He had not acted the gentleman that evening. He would have to make amends.

"What do you suggest I do?" he finally asked, his tone weary and resigned.

Cris did not like the glee shining in his friend's gaze, but there was nothing to be done. He trusted the duke not to reveal his humiliation, although he was sure to tease him about it in the future.

"You must send flowers. Since, if I remember correctly, last night would have been the young woman's first *ton* event, she will no doubt be on the receiving end of a number of such gifts, but you must not allow that to deter you. Nothing gets you back into a lady's good graces as quickly as a bouquet of flowers. If you could somehow ascertain her favourite flowers, that would be all the better."

The earl rolled his eyes. "This is all rather foolish, Wexford. It is not as though I wish to court the girl."

"Perhaps not, but you do wish to court her good opinion, do you not?"

Crispin thought that was still saying it a little too strong, but he grudgingly nodded.

"Excellent!" The duke rubbed his hands together, making the earl feel that he was getting far too much enjoyment over his predicament. "Now, tell me exactly what the chit said."

Crispin sighed once more but then conceded. "You would have enjoyed witnessing the exchange, to be sure. I would have thought her magnificent if all that rage was not directed at me. She wanted so badly to rip up at me, but Lady Vigilia prevented her from causing a scene. It would have been spectacular to watch her explode, but it was quite fascinating to watch her simmer as well."

The duke was watching him as though fascinated, much to Crispin's disgust. "Stop it, Wexford, I am definitely NOT in the market for a new countess, so you needn't look at me as though you know something. I am NOT falling for a debutante."

The duke shrugged. "If you say so, Crossley." He didn't sound convinced, but he moved on. "So, what you're saying is that you need to redeem yourself for your failure to be a gentleman with this lady, am I right?"

"That sums it up fairly well."

Nodding, the duke sank into thought, staring into his glass for a silent moment. "You need to help her with her quest."

"Now you're starting to sound like a medieval tale," Crispin scoffed.

The duke grinned but warmed to his subject. With a roll of his eyes he pressed on. "What does the chit want? Why is she here? To find a husband like all the other young women, no doubt," he answered his own question. "If you don't want her for yourself, you must ensure she finds a suitable husband to take care of her future."

Crispin could see the sense in the duke's words, but his stomach turned at the thought of it. "You think I ought to condemn some other man to be leg-shackled, in order to redeem myself? That hardly sounds gentlemanly."

"Most men do not consider matrimony to be the death sentence you think it," the duke replied drily. "Besides, did you not say the chit had merits?"

"She wasn't so bad as debutantes go," was as high as his praises would rise. "Have you any idea how to go about arranging a match for the girl?"

The duke shrugged. "How hard can it be? Mothers manage it every Season. Surely, we can figure it out."

Now the earl began to regain his sense of humour and chuckled. He thought the duke's reasoning might be faulty but agreed that it surely couldn't be that difficult.

"First thing you need to do is spend a little time with the girl and find out what she needs most from a match."

"Won't spending time with her give her false hopes for a match with me?"

"Did you not just tell me the girl has taken you in disgust?"

"That might not last too long." Crispin did not lack for ego. "But if it does, then she's not likely to agree to spend time with me."

"Lady Sherton is not going to allow her to refuse you, Crossley," the duke reminded him, beginning to become impatient. "Just be sure to tell the chit you are merely trying to make amends, not set up a flirtation."

"Somehow, I don't know if that will put me any further into her good graces, but I will take it under advisement. I see the merit in your plan. I do feel the need for redemption as I have never had such a lapse before."

The duke was finished with the topic, at least for the time being. "Very well, Crossley. Keep me apprised of your progress. I must be off. And you look as though you could use some rest," he observed with a sarcastic chuckle.

Crispin watched the duke walk from the room. He admired the other man's ability to control himself and others. It must be something to do with being a duke. While Crispin would love to be able to imitate the control the duke had, he wouldn't want the responsibility that accompanied the power. He had enough to do with his own earldom. And now he had Miss Holton on his conscience.

Chapter Nine

"Lord Crossley is here to see you, Miss." The butler had come himself, not bothering to send a footman, as though he knew he would be dropping an explosive into the room.

Vicky and Georgia exchanged shocked glances before turning to the countess.

"Well don't just sit there, girl, run to your room and make yourself presentable. It would not do to keep the earl waiting."

Georgia took a deep breath and held it while counting as quickly as possible to ten. She knew she couldn't tell the countess what she really thought, but surely she wouldn't be forced to accompany the dreadful man.

"I would prefer to abstain from seeing him, my lady."

"I beg your pardon?" The countess' tone made it clear she was not actually begging, nor did she seek pardon. "Has the earl compromised you?"

Hot colour flooded Georgia's cheeks. "Of course not."

"Then there is no reason to refuse to see him. I don't care a jot about this nonsense of you being an heiress. You girls have admitted that you are as much at fault as he is. Do not be missish. Any one of my daughters would give her pin money to be the one the earl is calling on. But for some inexplicable reason, he has asked for you. Do not demonstrate such a lack of gratitude that you will ignore the honour he is showing you. You have dithered quite long enough. Now, you haven't time to even go to your room and right yourself. You must go and see what the man wants."

Georgia was torn between fury and humiliation. Angry that the countess would spare no thought to her feelings and humiliated that she would say as much in front of her friends and the servants. She clenched her teeth and set her chin, refusing to be cowed by the aristocratic woman. Georgia knew her face was flaming, but she refused to hang her head. She followed the butler to the foyer where the earl stood gazing out a window. Georgia could only hope he hadn't heard the exchange. The countess' voice had not been raised, nor was it shrill, but sounds could carry quite easily in the large, high-ceilinged house.

For some inexplicable reason, Georgia's anger was merely fanned to greater heights by the fact that the earl was looking even more handsome than he had on previous occasions. The sun streaming in the window glinted off his chestnut hair, making it look soft and warm. She had never felt the impulse to touch another person's hair before, but she had to struggle to still her hand from reaching toward the cretin's head. When he turned to observe her, the sight of laughter dancing in his bright blue eyes made her anger flicker even higher. *Is he laughing at my attire or did he hear the countess' words?* She wanted to kick him in the shins and flee back to her village, but the countess' words rang in her ears. She could not show such ingratitude to the Shertons, nor could she abandon her dearest friend.

Swallowing all her pent-up emotions, Georgia strove to be polite. "You asked for me, my lord?" was the best she could do, but it was far better than the "What in tarnation do you want?" that she wished to say.

"Good afternoon, Miss Holton. I brought these for you." She hadn't even noticed that he was holding a small bouquet of rosebuds. They were the most delicate blush colour she had ever seen. There had been a steady stream of flowers being delivered to the house all day with four young women in residence, but in Georgia's opinion, these were the most beautiful ones to have entered the building.

Georgia didn't want to, but she felt her anger abating at the sight of such an offering. She made an effort to bolster it. "Do you think my forgiveness can be bought with flowers, my lord?" Her voice wasn't as cold as she would have wished, but at least the words were right.

"Not at all, Miss Holton, but I do hope you will at least give me a chance to try to redeem myself."

She knew she shouldn't trust him. His warm, reasonable tone was far too practiced, as though he were experienced with convincing young women not to hate him. Georgia sighed. She really didn't have much choice. Not that she was about to trust him or forgive him, but she had to see what else he wanted. He could have sent the flowers with a note. The fact that he was here in person told her there was more to it.

"What did you have in mind?" She almost smiled when she heard how guarded her voice sounded. At least she didn't sound like a pushover.

The earl bowed in front of her, much to her surprise. "I would beg the pleasure of your company for a ride in the Park. It is a remarkably fine afternoon."

Now, Georgia couldn't help her smile. At least she would be able to run to her room and right her appearance. It was bad enough that the earl had seen her like this, but there was no way she would gad about Town without at least running a comb through her curls.

"Very well, my lord, but I must ask you to wait for a few minutes while I get my bonnet."

"Of course. If it is fine with you, I will wait for you outside. I would rather not leave my horses standing much longer. They are a little high-strung, and the street is busy at this time of the day."

"That would probably be a good idea." She didn't bother offering further comment, merely turning on her heel and hurrying up the stairs as quietly and gracefully as she could, without a backward glance.

~~~

Crispin grinned at the butler after he tore his eyes from her retreating form. He admired her spunk if nothing else. At least the girl wasn't insipid. He knew he was in for an interesting afternoon. Realizing that standing in the foyer left him open to potentially having to speak to one or more of the Sherton sisters, the earl too turned on his heel and left the room.

He was just getting his matched bays turned around when Miss Holton appeared at the top of the stairs. Crispin almost stared. He had never known a woman who did not delight in keeping a man waiting. Especially when she was angry with him. And the chit looked remarkably appealing as she stood and gazed at him.

For the split of a second, he thought she looked hesitant and vulnerable but then dismissed the ridiculous thought. The girl could be a termagant when she wanted; he didn't think she had an uncertain bone in her body. He thrust the momentary compassionate feelings aside and reminded himself that he was merely here to assuage his guilt for breaking his word. She was a female, a noblewoman at that, and therefore not to be trusted. She didn't need his compassion and would probably scorn it if he were to offer it. He hardened his heart but tried to keep it from showing on his face.

After handing her up into his curricle, the girl sat prim and silent beside him. He was becoming uncomfortable with the silence and was thus goaded into speech.
~~~

"You are the promptest female I have ever met." It was the first thing that came to his mind to say.

"I beg your pardon?" She turned to him with startled eyes that suddenly filled with laughter. "I do apologize, my lord, I wasn't paying any heed to what you were saying. Surely you realize this is the first time I have ever ridden in a curricle. I do hope I wasn't doing anything so ill-bred as preening."

Crispin was astonished and couldn't prevent a bark of laughter. "No, I can assure you there was no preening. In fact, I was quite convinced that you were holding yourself stiff and silent due to your fury with me."

The girl grinned but then primly replied. "Well, I am still quite angry with you, but I will revive it only after I have absorbed the marvel of this experience. I mean, a curricle, my lord. If only my brothers were here to see me. I am trying to absorb every sensation so that I shan't forget anything when I write them about it. They will be pea green with envy, I can assure you."

Again, Crispin had to laugh. "Have you really never ridden in a curricle before?"

"Never. I've barely even seen one before. Remember, I live in a village. The most common conveyance I see on a regular basis is a gig. I don't think even Lord Sherton has a curricle. Last year they had a grand house party and a couple of the young gentlemen brought curricles, that is how I even know what they are. My brothers told me. They aren't the most practical of vehicles, I will admit, but it is quite lovely to ride in it. So, I cannot be angry with you just at the moment, you understand."

"So, you are the sort that holds a grudge." He stated this fact, not asking.

"Not usually, no, but your transgression was rather large, my lord. But, please, let us not ruin this lovely afternoon with such talk."

"Do you wish for silence?" Crispin had never met a woman who didn't want to talk his ears off when she wasn't giving him the silent treatment.

"If you don't mind, my lord. It'll be all the better for me to know what to write to the boys." Her apologetic tone made him want to laugh again, but he managed to keep a straight face.

"Of course. I shall save my comments for later then."

They continued in silence until they were halfway down Rotten Row. Then the chit offered a heartfelt sigh and turned to him with a grin.

"This is really quite lovely, my lord. I suppose it would be rather churlish to hold onto my anger toward you considering this stupendous experience you have afforded me. How did you know to bring a curricle? Or am I being decidedly provincial by remarking on it? I suppose most debutantes would expect it, or at least it would not be the very first time they'd ever ridden in one." Her next sigh was not nearly so full of delight, in fact, it sounded almost despondent.

"Actually, Miss Holton, now that I think on it, if I had been thinking clearly, I would not have brought my curricle."

Her gasp of dismay made him smile before continuing. "That is not to say that I wish to deprive you of the experience, but I just remembered that there have been a few ladies that are terrified of riding in a curricle. If I had thought the matter through carefully, I would have brought a safer vehicle."

"Well, then I am relieved that you were thoughtless," she said with a laugh. "Why would they be afraid? It does not seem unsafe to me."

"Me neither, but there have been some accidents, especially if the driver is inexperienced."

"Well, there you have it. I would never expect anyone to describe you as inexperienced. You have probably been riding since before you could walk and driving nearly as long."

Her approving tone made the earl want to preen. She certainly knew how to talk to males. *Her brothers must love her*, he thought with wry humour.

"Do your brothers ride and drive?"

"Of course. But nothing so grand as your pair."

They continued in more companionable silence for a few moments while Crispin wondered uncomfortably how to raise the subject of her quest. He shook his head again at the duke's whimsical wording.

He took a deep breath and plunged into the topic. "I feel dreadful about breaking your confidence, Miss Holton, and wish to make amends. What can I do to make it up to you?"

Crispin had to fight not to squirm when she turned her searching gaze onto him. She appeared amazed by his words and looked like she wanted to read all his secrets from his face.

"You must be the oldest sibling," he blurted out.

She trilled a laugh. "Why do you say that?"

"You have the air about you as though you can read my thoughts just from examining my face."

"Well, you are certainly more inscrutable than any of my brothers or sisters." Her disgruntled tone made him smile before she continued. "You are right. I *am* the oldest. Which means all the responsibility rests upon me. Most of them are much younger than I am. My closest sibling, Gregory, ran off to war as soon as he turned fifteen. But the rest of us are at home. I've pretty much had to raise them since my mama died bringing Drew into the world seven years ago. So yes, I've learned there's much to be read in someone's face. Especially guilty boys."

She had tried to turn it back into a jest, but he could see the emotion shining in her eyes over the losses she had felt.

"Seven years ago, you must have been little more than a child yourself," he couldn't help from prying.

"I was almost thirteen. Many boys and girls have already gone into service by that age," she dismissed his sympathy with a slight wave of her hand. "There was no other option, anyway, and this way I could pass on to them what Mama had already taught me." She averted her face for a moment before turning back to him with a jaunty grin. "But never mind about that, my lord, you were saying something about wanting to make amends for your lapse in gentlemanly behaviour. This sounds intriguing. What do you think you could possibly do to make amends?"

"I could help you with your purpose for being in London for the Season." He stated this with as much firmness as he could muster, despite his own misgivings about this "quest" and the derision he could see in her gleaming eyes.

"That might be a challenge for you, my lord, since you know nothing about my purpose for being in London."

"Are you not here seeking a husband like every other young lady?"

"Well, I am not a lady, you will recall, my lord, I am merely a miss, for one thing. And no, I am not here seeking a mate. Even if I were, your little lapse made it impossible anyway, so it is just as well that I was merely expecting a diverting holiday with my dearest friend."

Crispin felt his stomach drop with what felt like dismay over her words. "What do you mean I made it impossible? How can it being known that you are an heiress make it impossible? You will have to be more discerning, of course, which I can help you with, in order to steer you away from the fortune hunters."

Her tinkling laughter did nothing to settle the queasy sensation.

"Do not trouble yourself about it, my lord. I absolve you. You needn't make any effort at redemption. I shall be perfectly fine. I am here to help Vicky have fun this Season. That is all. After two weeks, I will return home to the life that is waiting for me in our village with jolly memories to last me for years. And when Vicky writes to me, which she so often does, I will now have faces to put to the names and places she mentions. It is as simple as that. So, you did not disrupt anything. That was the plan all along."

There was a pause while Crispin tried to digest what she had said. Her earnest expression led him to believe she was telling the truth as she saw it, but he was struggling to believe her. The fact that she was not meeting his gaze did not help his unease. But suddenly she interrupted his musings.

"My lord, do you know that child?" She was discretely pointing toward a small boy that was running toward their curricle while waving.

Crispin had to bite his tongue to prevent every unclean word he knew from leaving his lips. *The governess is going to be let off without a single grout*, he thought viciously as he slapped the reins to goad his horses into a trot. He gritted his teeth as his companion gasped and grabbed the edge of her seat.

"What is the matter with you? Are you running away from a child?" Her incredulity made him grimace.

"He should know better than to accost me."

"He was a *child*." She put heavy emphasis on the last word. "He could no more accost you than could a kitten."

"Kittens have claws, Miss Holton."

"Perhaps they do, but they aren't going to do much damage to a grown man. And that child did not look like just any urchin. He was well dressed, and while I didn't see much after you almost upended me from your curricle, it looked to me as though he were being chased by a governess. Perhaps he was the son of one of your friends and merely wanted to say hello or admire your handsome horses."

"He doesn't belong to any of my friends."

"How do you know?"

"He belongs to me." The heavy silence that met his statement made him glance over at her. The chit had such a look of disapproval written all over her face from the furrow between her brows to the tight line her lips were pulled into that Crispin instantly knew he was in for another one of her tirades.

"I would like to get off now, please, my lord." Her polite words were barely audible as though she had to force them through her clenched teeth.

He was surprised. "Do you wish to stroll?"

"No, my lord, I find your company distasteful, and I no longer wish to share it. I would rather walk all the way back to Sherton than spend another moment in your handsome curricle if you are also in it."

The earl had never been so politely but coldly insulted in all his life. "I am not leaving you on your own in Hyde Park, Miss Holton. You will have to bear with my presence until I can escort you back to your home."

"I believe I would be better off on my own. Please, stop this carriage right this minute." She had been keeping her voice quiet at first, but by the end of her statement it had begun to rise.

When he still did not pull his horses to a stop, she shifted her position, and he realized she was about to jump. He shifted all the reins to his right hand and grabbed her arm before she could. He held onto her tightly while he pulled over beside a copse of trees.

"Are you insane? You could get killed trying such a stunt." He wanted to shake her and bellow at her, but in an effort not to draw attention he merely hissed the words but kept his hold on her arm.

"Let go of me," she hissed back. "If you do not want me causing an uncomfortable scene, you will remove your hand from my person and allow me to get down from this ridiculous carriage."

"Ridiculous carriage?" he shot back. "Just moments ago, you were preening over the adventure of riding in my best curricle."

"That was before I realized you are a charlatan. I want nothing to do with you, and I feel tainted just by being in your presence. Let me go, Crossley," she insisted.

"I really cannot leave a madwoman to run about on her own in Hyde Park. I will escort you back to the Shertons and let them deal with you."

"I am not the mad one here, my lord. I am not the one who just ran away from his own son."

"Who said anything about him being my son?"

"You said he belonged to you."

"There could be a vast difference between the two."

"Whatever the difference might be, it is quite mad to run away from a child, my lord. He couldn't have been much more than four or five years of age. Clearly, he meant you no harm whatever the case of his parentage might be. And in either case, I no longer wish to share your presence. Please, unhand me and allow me to make my own way home."

Chapter Ten

Georgia was seething and could barely sit still. She didn't want to draw too much attention to herself and thus shame the Shertons, but she would have loved to kick and scream at the wicked earl. How he was accepted by everyone was beyond her. He was certainly no gentleman. If this was what the *ton* was like, she was rather relieved that he had made it impossible for her to remain there. She shuddered at the thought of being married to a man like him and began to worry about her dear Vicky's future.

"Come, Miss Holton, you know I cannot just leave you here. You must see reason."

The earl's low voice and his attempts at soothing her were having the opposite effect. She would so enjoy hitting him with her parasol if she had thought to bring one with her.

"Reason? Really, my lord? You want me to see reason? You are the one who claims to have possession of a child but then ran away from him. And you are also the one who cannot keep his word or hold a confidence. I am a perfectly amiable young woman who would like to go my own way unaccosted by one such as you. I do not need to see reason."

When the earl chuckled suddenly Georgia truly began to fear for her safety. She had thought the man a touch irregular, but now she truly questioned his sanity. Her feelings must have written themselves on her face because he held up his free hand in a staying motion.

"I know, laughing at this moment does not reassure you, I am sure. But your righteous indignation is a sight to behold, my dear Miss Holton, and I could not help myself. I swear to you, I am not a madman. I will drive you straight back to Lady Sherton and shan't darken your door without an invitation ever again."

Georgia wouldn't trust the man farther then she could throw him and, considering his size, that would not be very far. But he wasn't wrong about the fact that she could not just traipse around the city on her own. Since the earl was driving a curricle, she hadn't been able to bring a maid with her, so if she left him she would do so alone.

"Please, return me to the Shertons immediately, my lord." She couldn't bypass almost two decades of training to be polite, but even though she said please it was through tight lips and in a steely tone.

She heard him sigh but refused to look at the earl. Georgia didn't think she had herself well enough in hand not to start shrilling at him like a fishwife if she set eyes on him at that moment. *Why did I agree to take a ride with him?* She could have politely refused or even claimed a headache. The countess had merely insisted that she see why he was calling; she hadn't said Georgia had to accompany him. But she was honest enough to admit, at least to herself, that part of her had thrilled at the thought of going for a drive at the fashionable hour in Hyde Park, where everyone would see that she was not such a bumpkin that she could not receive an invitation from one such as he. So really, she wasn't much better than he was. In London for not even two full days and already she was being influenced by its questionable standards.

She was grateful that he didn't insist on trying for polite conversation. Or impolite, for that matter. Since she had seen fit to let him know what she thought of him, one couldn't argue that she had been perfectly polite. Her stomach was beginning to hurt, but she was glad to see that he made short work of turning them around and getting them safely back to her lodging. Thankfully, it wasn't far to Curzon Street. The girls would, of course, wonder why she was back so soon, but she couldn't find it in herself to care at that moment. She was certain it wouldn't harm them in any way. Besides, they were better off not having any association with the mad earl anyway. Georgia offered up a silent wish that she not have to see the man for the rest of her stay in London.

~~~

Her wish proved to be futile.

The earl dropped her off with a stiff farewell and helped her down from the curricle. She nodded acknowledgement of his words and then nearly fled into the house.

"Miss Holton, we had not thought to see you for at least another half hour or more," the surprised butler commented, making heat flood Georgia's cheeks.

"We did not drive as far as expected," was all she had to offer. "Are the ladies still in the drawing room?"

"No, Miss. Lady Rosabel has gone driving, Lady Hilaria is in her room, I believe, and Lady Sherton and Lady Vigilia have gone out to make some calls before the evening's entertainments."

"Thank you, Mr. Jennings. I will be in Lady Vigilia's room resting before this evening."

The butler sketched her a brief bow. Georgia had the sinking feeling that the man was disappointed in her, but there was little she could do about it. It would embarrass them both if she tried to explain herself, besides the fact that she ought not to be gossiping with the Shertons' servants. And the only explanation she could offer was that the earl belonged in
~~~

Bedlam. Lady Sherton would not thank her for bandying that around.

With as much dignity as she could muster, Georgia made her way up to the room she was sharing with Vicky. A part of her wanted to pack her luggage and head back to the village. But that would be the coward's way out. And she didn't want to do that to Vicky, who seemed so delighted to have her here. Georgia sighed again as she threw herself onto the high bed. She needed to take a moment to regain her perspective.

Staring at the ceiling Georgia marvelled, *even the ceilings are ornate here!* She shoved the inconsequential thought out of her mind.

"It is quite lovely not to be the one in charge of the household for a change. I ought to be enjoying the vacation. And I truly do want to see the city. It would be lovely to go to some bookshops, and milliners, and even to Tattersall's. I must ask if they allow women there. And the theatre, I really must get to the theatre. Besides the fact that there are so many more people to meet. If I am to follow Vicky's letters in the future, it behooves me to meet as many of her acquaintances as possible. Perhaps I will even be introduced to her future husband. I cannot allow the words and actions of one crazed man to send me running from Town." She sat up abruptly, and her gaze collided with her own reflection in the mirror across the room. "In fact, he would be winning if I left now. That will just not do." Her conviction solidified. "I shall merely cast him from my mind. He is nothing to me. It matters little what he says, does, or thinks. I needn't give him another thought."

Just as she was concluding, Vicky burst into the room. "Who were you talking to?"

Georgia flushed with hot colour. "Myself," she said with a sheepish grin.

Vicky laughed. "Well, you are the best one to talk to. But what are you doing back? I would have thought a ride in Hyde Park would take considerably longer."

"Oh, we didn't go very far. The earl just wanted to apologize once more for breaking our confidence. After I accepted his apology, we didn't have much else to say to one another so he brought me back here."

She had to work hard not to squirm under Vicky's questioning gaze. Thankfully, although she looked sceptical, all Vicky had to say was, "I've never known you to be at a loss for words."

Georgia forced out a laugh. "No, it is a rare occurrence, that is true. But never mind about that. What have you been doing? And what are we going to be doing tonight?"

This was the perfect distraction. Vicky happily launched into a long description of the visits they had made. "If only we had known your drive with Crossley wasn't going to result in much, it would have been better for you to accompany us on our visits. You would have enjoyed them far more."

"Well there's always next time," Georgia murmured, glad that her friend hadn't pressed for more information. She normally told Vicky everything, but she was unusually reluctant to tell her about her strange afternoon and the earl's bizarre behaviour.

"You are absolutely correct, my friend, now let me ring for the maid to bring us some water so we can begin our preparations for the evening. Tonight will be your first ball, and we must make sure everything is perfect."

Georgia couldn't remain in her dull mood for long in the face of Vicky's excitement to be sharing the joys of the Season with her. Before long they were engrossed in preparations, and in what felt like the blink of an eye they were on their way to the ball.

Despite her disquieting afternoon, Georgia couldn't help but join in with Vicky's enthusiasm. She certainly wouldn't consider herself to be a slave to fashion, in fact, she had never worn anything considered remotely fashionable in her life and it had never bothered her. But here, in London, with Vicky, she found herself falling under the spell of the beautiful clothes and the stylishly adorned hair. She was beginning to realize it would be harder to leave this behind than she had thought. But there was no other option. She had responsibilities back in the village, and there could be nothing for her here in London save these two weeks as Vicky's companion. It would have to do. And it would have to stay here in London. She would not allow it to haunt her after she returned home. But she would milk every last drop of enjoyment from it that she could while she was here.

This last thought traipsed through her mind as their carriage came to a stop in front of the large, elegant house where they would be spending the next couple of hours. Georgia marvelled at the fact that their evening was just beginning when most people in the village would be taking to their beds. She shook her head with amazement as she stepped down from the carriage.

She realized she would have to work hard not to stare around like a bumpkin. Despite her exposure to the Shertons, as well as the little bit of experience she had so far enjoyed while here in London, she hadn't been prepared for the overwhelming beauty of a ballroom packed to overflowing with the fashionable elite. Each person her eyes landed on seemed to be better dressed than the previous. And it seemed to Georgia that every second lady was being dragged down by an overabundance of jewels. Thieves would have a real frolic if ever they could find their way into such an event, she thought rather contemptuously. *Why would anyone want to wear quite so many jewels at the same time? Have they no care for their own safety? Or do they perhaps believe they are so very important that no one would dare accost them?*

Georgia stifled a sigh. She was not so unaffected by her afternoon as she had thought. She realized her sarcastic thoughts were unkind, and she forced a smile to her lips when she encountered the next overly bejeweled lady that Vicky wanted her to meet.

"How do you do?" the other woman murmured politely.

"Very well, thank you. It is a pleasure to meet you," Georgia replied, although she had already forgotten the woman's name. She called herself to task and tried to focus.

"I have heard you are the young heiress that is staying with the Shertons this Season."

Georgia felt heat climbing into her cheeks and floundered for a reply. Really, it wasn't even a question, so what could she say?

She tried to smile pleasantly, but she wasn't sure if she pulled it off. She looked to Vicky for help, but her friend looked as perplexed as she felt. Finally, she cleared her throat and said, "I am enjoying the pleasure of being a guest of the Shertons for a few weeks here in London, but I fear you are mistaken if you think I am an heiress, my lady. I am merely a friend of the family here for a short visit."

"Oh, you needn't be coy with me, Miss Holton. There is no shame in inheriting funds. In fact, you ought to be proud of it."

Georgia could only blink and smile at the woman. It was worse than they had thought. It would seem she was the talk of the *ton* for all the wrong reasons. There was nothing she could do but make the most of it. Perhaps it would be diverting. She allowed her smile to widen as she bowed her head to the older woman. Without a word, she dipped into a curtsy knowing full well the woman would take it as acquiescence. Thankfully, though, it also served the purpose of ending the awkward conversation. With a smile at the younger women, the lady turned to hail some other acquaintances.

"Why did you smile at her like that? She is more convinced than ever that you are some rich female nabob. Now what shall you do?" Vicky's wide-eyed stare only brought on a giggle from Georgia.

"What else could I do, Vick? The woman was already convinced because she heard it from someone she believes more than me. Since the mad earl opened his traitorous mouth, there has been no one interested in the truth of the matter. To them, I am an heiress. We might as well go with it as there's nothing that can be done. It might even prove amusing to see which of the fortune hunters will be the first to present themselves to your father." She had been speaking as quietly as possible while continuing to gaze about, but her last words caused her to turn to Vicky, aghast. "Do you think we ought to tell your father what has happened? Your mother didn't seem too upset over our story, but we should warn your father, at least, that he is sure to be fielding some bizarre interest in your temporary guest."

Vicky giggled. "You're right, it is a funny predicament. But I cannot decide if we should tell my father or not. He is sure to be displeased with us over it. Mother already knows about it and rang a peel over my head. I can only imagine what will happen if all the fortune hunters start making a path to our door."

Georgia clenched her teeth at the injustice. "It is certainly not our fault. That simpleton Crossley is to blame."

Vicky shrugged. "You and I both know that, but in my experience, I am always the one who takes the blame. I don't see how this will be any different."

"Well, let's never mind about it for now. We are at a ball, and it is bound to be far more interesting than worrying about what we cannot control."

Vicky's spirits appeared to revive over those words, and a grin broke over her face. Georgia set her mind to enjoying the evening. Thankfully, it didn't appear as though it was going to be very difficult. Before too long, the girls were surrounded by young men clamouring for an introduction or requesting their hands for the next dance. It would seem they were not to be wallflowers that night. Georgia was gratified.

Until her gaze collided with Lord Crossley's from across the room and all the air seeped out of her lungs. She was in the middle of a cotillion, for which she was grateful. She was so familiar with the steps that she managed not to trip or otherwise draw attention to herself.

He was standing on the side of the dance floor talking with another gentleman, but his eyes followed her as she circled the room through the steps of the dance. After that breathless moment, she had managed to drag her eyes away from his and her attention back to her dance partner, but she could feel his focus on her and the fine hairs on the back of her neck stood at attention while a small frisson shivered its way down her back.

~~~

The chit was here, just as he had expected. Crispin allowed his gaze to follow her as she moved through the crowded dance floor in the arms of Lord Tipton. Crispin could feel his jaw tighten when it registered in his mind who her partner was. The man wasn't a bounder by any means, but it was a well-known fact that he needed to marry into money to save his estates from falling into ruin.

Cris kept watching the Holton girl. She was a taking little thing. But he had never allowed a debutante to ensnare his attention since he had been fool enough to fall for Cassandra. He supposed it was his shame over breaking his word that kept him uncharacteristically focused on the young woman. And he could now understand a little bit of why she was so angry. By
~~~

breaking his word, it seemed he had opened her up to being pursued by all the fortune hunters. Of course, that was the usual state of affairs of any heiress, so he didn't really understand why she was so determined to avoid that fate. Most of the tonnish busybodies would have ferreted out the information of her finances anyway. Did she not expect Lady Sherton to have divulged it anyway, even if he had kept his silence?

Crispin called himself to task. That was no excuse for his own lapse in judgment. He had to make it up to her despite the mess he had made of his attempt that afternoon. Not that there was anything truly wrong with Tipton, but he was a dullard and would not do for the spirited young Holton girl. He would have to make sure she met some more appropriate gentlemen. But who? And really, was this not Lady Sherton's responsibility? Crispin rolled his eyes at his own foolishness.

But just in that instant his gaze collided with Georgia's once more, and for an instant he could see that she looked stricken. Crispin cursed under his breath. He was going to have to ask the chit to dance. He made his way through the sea of people.

He reached them just as Tipton was escorting her back to Lady Vigilia's side.

"Miss Holton, might I request your hand for the next dance?"

Despite the fact that her voice did not sound in the least regretful, the chit answered, "I am sorry to have to tell you that I do not think I have a single dance left uncommitted this evening, my lord."

"Then might I have the pleasure of escorting you in to supper, or have you committed that already as well?"

He could see that she wished to deny him but was surprised by her reluctant honesty. "No, my lord, I have not yet been asked."

"Very well, then I shall have the pleasure."

She dipped into a shallow curtsy in response, not bothering to use any words, but her lack of enthusiasm was expressed loud and clear. He wanted to grin. The chit was amusing in all her prickly little kitten efforts.

There was no time for any further conversation as both girls were then claimed by their promised partners as the next dance was starting up. Not wanting to make a cake of himself and have it become obvious to anyone that he was singling out the Holton girl, Crispin set himself to the task of partnering a couple other girls before it was time for supper. He knew it would surprise the nosy onlookers to see him on the dance floor, but he was relieved to find some of the less annoying ladies who still had spaces to fill on their dance cards.

He would never for the life of him properly understand why some ladies became so popular and others remained wallflowers. The two girls he partnered were perfectly articulate and sufficiently graceful. He wondered momentarily why either of them were in London for their second season. Not that he particularly cared either way, he reminded himself. He had no intention of raising expectations in the hearts of any young ladies by asking such a question.

Finally, it was time to find Miss Holton and escort her to supper. Crispin hoped he would be able to seat her at a table for two and have an actual conversation with her in which neither of them grew angry. Luck was on his side. She followed him meekly enough as he filled both their plates and spied the perfect table off to the side of the room. She didn't say anything, but her face said enough despite her apparent effort to remain impassive. He smiled at her, trying to keep the grin from his face.

"Thank you for agreeing to eat with me. I didn't think you would after this afternoon."

Colour rose in her cheeks. "You didn't ask if I wanted to accompany you, my lord. You asked if I had a partner for supper. I couldn't avoid an honest answer."

He quirked an eyebrow at her. "Is honesty important to you?" He tried to keep sarcasm from his tone, but he wasn't perfectly successful. Her colour heightened.

"Of course it is, my lord, which is why I am so uncomfortable with people discussing my inheritance."

Now Crispin was confused. "What do you mean? Isn't it dishonesty that is wanting you to keep it a secret?"

"Not at all."

Crispin stared across the table at the girl. She stopped picking at her food and looked back at him, straight in the eye. Despite her heightened colour, he could see no guile in her face. The chit was being honest with him.

"Could you explain yourself?"

The girl sighed. "I don't mean to be rude to you, my lord, but I don't have any obligation to explain myself to you. I could ask you to explain yourself about all sorts of things, but they are really none of my business, so I am restraining myself."

Crispin chuckled. "And I ought to do the same, is that what you mean?"

She offered him a lopsided grin and a little shrug followed by a nod.

"Well, perhaps we can exchange information. What sorts of things would you wish me to explain?"

He was amused to watch her surprise. He had clearly caught her attention and surprised her with his offer. She bit her lip and searched his face. He felt his gut clench in response. She really was a pretty young woman, if one was at all interested in unmarried, young debutantes, which he most certainly was not, he reminded himself.

"There are any number of things, my lord, which are none of my business but which interest me. Why did you tell Lord Layton what we had divulged in confidence? And why are you so angry about that boy who is your ward? Really, why do you almost always appear to be angry?" She trailed off into a whisper as she asked her last question. Crispin supposed he must be looking particularly angry again, and he tried to paste a more pleasant aspect to his face. He doubted he was very successful as she continued to chew her lip worriedly.

Forcing his gaze away from her lips, he contemplated her questions. None of them would be easy to answer. And really, none of his answers would be appropriate for the ears of an innocent debutante. But he was now unreservedly curious about her inheritance and wish for secrecy. But giving voice to her questions, she had tacitly agreed to tell him if he satisfied her curiosity. Unfortunately, they were not the type of shallow questions he was hoping for.

He tried for a sterilized answer to her questions. "I don't have an answer for why I spoke to Layton. I don't even like the bounder. It just slipped out of my mouth, for which I am profoundly sorry." She kept herself remarkably contained, not displaying much reaction to his words beyond a slight nod of her head, which he found mildly fascinating. He wouldn't be able to explain why, but he quite liked the girl and was uncomfortable with the thought of being in her bad graces. He was relieved by her small nod and even more so when she appeared a trifle more comfortable and took a small bite of her food.

He felt heat rise into his cheeks as he swallowed and continued to answer her questions. "The answer to your second two questions stem from the same source. My wife."

Now she betrayed a reaction as she blinked rapidly and almost choked on the bite she had been in the process of swallowing. "Your wife, my lord?" she repeated as a question before continuing. "I thought you were a bachelor."

"I am, or rather a widower." His answer was stark. "But my wife caused me a great deal of trouble. That boy was hers. Since he was born during our marriage, legally he is mine."

She regarded him steadily with a slight frown between her brows. He enjoyed watching her think but was unprepared for the blaze of anger that crossed her features.

"I take it from your words that your wife was unfaithful to you." She said the words in a matter of fact tone, but he could see from her heightened colour that she was uncomfortable, though she continued anyway. "But that can hardly be the child's fault, can it my lord? Despite how despicable your dead wife might have been, she is still dead, and therefore has paid for her sins, would you not agree? And now you are compounding them for that poor child by effectively making him an orphan."

She paused briefly. "You didn't tell me his name. It feels terrible to keep saying boy or child."

Crispin stared at her. "Christopher," he nearly growled the word.

She carried on. "If you were going to denounce Christopher, would the time of his birth not have been the appropriate time? The fact that he is yours, as you say, means that you ought to be treating him in the manner that befits your heir, which he is legally. It seems to me as though you treat your cattle better than you are treating that little boy. In fact, since you have been at such pains to beg my forgiveness, you are treating me, a complete stranger, better than him." She kept her voice low, and her face did not betray her intent to any observers, but her tone dripped with disdain. "No wonder you are an angry man. You are being very unnatural."

Crispin felt hostility rise within him. "I rather think it is quite natural to be angry over my wife's actions."

"That may well be, but it is not that poor child's fault." She was implacable in her determination to find fault with him. She made to rise. He grabbed her wrist, gently but firmly preventing her escape.

"Not so fast, my girl. I told you what you wanted to know. You might think I'm a dastard, but you cannot leave just yet."

She regarded him, her gaze steady and cold before a low chuckle escaped her. "Very well, my lord. You are correct in your assumption of my assessment of you, so I have no idea why you care to know, but I will answer your question."

She paused, took a deep breath, looked around the crowded room then continued in a low tone. "I did not want you to tell anyone about my inheritance because by *ton* standards it is infinitesimal, as I already mentioned to you. In our village, about twenty years ago, dear Mr. Byram had accumulated a small fortune but had no heirs, so he left it to the town with clear instructions on how it was to be disbursed. Most of it was to go to the school for boys' education, but some was set aside to provide a dowry of ten pounds to any girl who had lived in the village for seven years or more. I am to benefit from his bequest. So, you see, I am an heiress, but since it is ten pounds, it doesn't count here. So, Lady Vigilia was not lying. But I certainly did not want anyone to know of it. In this context, ten pounds is worse than nothing."

Crispin was struck to the core. He found her embarrassed puff of dismay to be adorable. Despite her momentary silence, apparently, she was not finished slicing into him with her gentle, resolute tone.

"So, you must now see, my lord, when you offered this afternoon to help me find a husband, why I said it was impossible because of what you said. Even if I wanted to find a mate in my two weeks here, I no longer can. Because the *ton* thinks I'm an heiress, it is now only the fortune hunters expressing interest. When the truth comes out, I will be seen as an imposter and will not be able to show my face."

"I am profoundly sorry, my dear girl."

She offered a shrug. "Do not trouble yourself. I did not come to Town with the intention of marrying, so you did not really rob me of anything. I will stick to my plan of having an entertaining two weeks with my dearest friend and then return to my simple life in the village. With my ten pounds, I will be able to find a hard-working husband and we can make a comfortable life for ourselves and my siblings. It is very simple and far different from what the *ton* might be familiar with, but it will fill my needs and is all that I ever expected from life. In fact, more than I expected. It wasn't until five months ago that I found out that I qualified for the bequest, and I was despairing about what I could do to care for my brothers and sisters."

The earl could only stare at her. He had never met such a reasonable young woman. The sensation of guilt rose to choke him. What could one say to the chit after what she had just revealed? His anger at her judgment over the boy was forgotten. She was obviously a better moral judge than he was. She was entitled to her opinion.

Chapter Eleven

"You must allow me to help you at least make your stay in Town memorable, if nothing else."

Crossley didn't trust the shrewd expression that fell over Georgia's face, but he did not allow his gaze to waver.

"It could be said that you have already done that," she said with a wry twist of her lips before she added, "You could take me driving in the Park again, I suppose, my lord."

"Of course, it would be my pleasure," he quickly said, surprised that her request would be so simple. He had spoken too soon.

"With the child, of course," she added with an evil twinkle in her eye. "I find I am sadly missing the company of children, and you are the only one I know that has one."

Crispin clenched his jaw. He wanted to growl at her but managed to keep his tone polite. "Perhaps you ought to volunteer some time at the foundling hospital if you are lonely for the company of small children."

Her gurgle of laughter caused his stomach to clench in an exceptionally different reaction than that over her words. She was a remarkably good-looking young woman, if you could ignore her managing ways. He shoved the ridiculous thought to the back of his mind when she again spoke.

With her amusement still dancing in her eyes, the chit shook her head. "Were you not looking for a way to assuage your guilt, my lord? This would be the ideal way, I should think – help me feel less lonely for the company of children and help that poor child to feel a little less neglected."

"He is far from neglected. I hire the very best of care for him."

She shrugged. "But he has no parents. How old were you when you lost your parents?"

He stared at her for a moment before answering stiffly. "I was twenty-one when my father died and twenty-five when I lost my mother."

"I'm sorry for your loss, my lord," she answered softly, obviously regretting her conversation choice but continuing valiantly. "Can you imagine if that had happened to you as a small child?" She paused for a moment, obviously hoping he would think about it. "I was thirteen when I lost my mother, and it was a terrible blow, but I know it was even worse for my brothers and sisters who were much younger. And we at least had each other." She paused again, taking a deep breath before launching into speech once again.

Crispin braced himself for what was to come; he could tell from her demeanour that she was about to launch an attack he would not enjoy.

"That boy may not be your son. You may be rightfully angry with his mother. But neither of those things are his fault. He is your responsibility, as you have freely admitted. You are not dispensing with your responsibility in an acceptable manner. Surely you realize that. He needs your time and attention. And it will make me feel ever so much better about being in London, my lord."

Despite his antipathy toward the boy and her words, the earl couldn't help laughing over her conclusion. The managing little baggage knew just what to say to prevent him from refusing.

With a sigh he finally said, "Very well. Shall I come to collect you at four or five tomorrow afternoon?"

She grinned. "Four might be best, my lord. We wouldn't want to overwhelm the boy with too many crowds." She paused before adding, her eyes twinkling, "Besides, if we find we are having a good time, that will afford us time to go to Gunther's for an ice before you return me home."

"Now you really are pushing it too far, my dear girl," he said, but there was little heat in his words. He accepted defeat gallantly. "Very well, the boy and I shall collect you at four."

"I shall look forward to it," she replied, polite but not necessarily truthful, although Crispin couldn't really tell. While she didn't appear to have warmed up to him too much, she seemed genuinely delighted by the thought of spending time with the child. Crispin almost laughed again. He never would have considered using the boy to appeal to women. Not that he wanted the attentions of any particular woman, he reminded himself wryly. He would have to keep reminding himself of that if he was going to be spending any amount of time with this particularly appealing young woman.

She rose to her feet and glanced around the room. "I fear I have monopolized your time, my lord."

Crispin was amused at her way of always turning the conversation in a self-deprecating way. He wondered what made her do that. If anyone overheard they would never know that he had to coerce her into spending time with him. It was one more thing he liked about her. He quickly got to his feet and offered his elbow to escort her back to the ballroom. He needn't chronicle all the things he liked about her. She was still a woman, even if she hadn't been guilty of the particular piece of deception he had thought. He gave his head a slight shake. He needed to get this woman out of his mind. He tried to keep his pace even. It would not do to be seen rushing her from the room.

The rest of the evening seemed to drag as he watched Miss Holton be handed from gentleman to lord. Georgia didn't spend a single dance on the sidelines. Her wide smile demonstrated how delighted she was with the attention. But he was honest enough to acknowledge that she wasn't simpering or flirting. The chit seemed to be an actual genuinely cheerful soul. From all appearances, her interest in each person she encountered was sincere. She was not flattering the men she danced with when she focused her intelligent gaze upon them as they spoke. But he could tell from their reactions that they were basking in her attention. That, combined with her supposed fortune, would ensure the girl multiple offers of marriage.

Several inappropriate expressions crossed his mind, and he had to clamp his jaw to prevent them from escaping his mouth. She was right. He had made it impossible for her to marry. No matter what she might say to the contrary, he couldn't believe that wouldn't have helped her situation. Despite the brave face she put on it, he couldn't see how marrying a bumpkin from her village would be better for her and her siblings than marrying a member of the *ton*. On second thought, not every male member of the *ton* would be a step up from the country bumpkin, but surely financially speaking it would be better for her. He stifled a sigh and tore his gaze away from her. What she surely didn't need was even more gossip about her! He dragged his focus away, not wanting anyone to notice his fixation.

To be on the safe side, he ought to ask some ladies to dance. He saw Vicky nearby and approached her.

"Might I have the privilege of dancing with you, my lady?"

Vicky's giggle only grated on his nerves slightly. "I'm sorry, my lord. My dance card is full tonight." She paused and looked around before continuing. "But my sister might be available, if you're just looking for a partner."

Crispin felt his eyebrows rising at her forwardness. She giggled at his expression.

"Was that inappropriate, my lord? I apologize, if I offended you." She didn't look particularly contrite as she turned with a smile to the gentleman waiting to escort her to the dance floor.

With a shrug, Crispin turned and looked for whom else he could ask to dance. He had no intention of following Vicky's suggestion. Hilaria was a chore to be around, and he had no desire to raise expectations with Lady Rosabel.

Eventually, much to his relief, he was able to make good his escape. He had danced with a couple young women whose names he could not recall and then took his leave of his hostess before making his way to his club. He was in dire need of a strong drink and the bracing company of other determined bachelors.

Georgia had tried to ignore her awareness of the earl as she danced through the rest of the ball, but she had felt a little deflated when he left the room. She refused to call the sensation jealousy when she had watched him dance with other girls. It would be unreasonable to be jealous, considering she had refused him herself. She made every effort to push him from her mind, but she wasn't very successful. Even though she continued to dance after he had left, the evening had gone slightly flat. She had no explanation for the strange phenomenon.

"Did you see Lord Crossley ask me to dance?" Vicky asked when they finally climbed up to her room in the wee hours of the morning.

Georgia grinned. "I did," she said with a giggle. "I also saw that you refused him."

Vicky giggled along with her but explained, "I didn't do it to be difficult. I really didn't have any dances available." She twirled around the room. "I knew having you here would be the best. I haven't enjoyed a ball as much as this evening."

Georgia couldn't hide her surprise. "Truly, Vicky? While it was lovely, I didn't see that it was so very spectacular."

Vicky guffawed. "Just a couple days here in Town and you're already as blasé as the rest of the debutantes."

Feeling heat creep up her cheeks, Georgia tried to explain. "I'm not trying to be blasé, my dear friend, and well you know it, but surely there have been better nights in all your times during the Season."

"Nope, not better than this." Georgia's gaze must have still been sceptical because Vicky hurried to add, "For one thing, I've never had my best friend in attendance. Add to that the fact that I almost never have my entire dance card filled, and you have the recipe for the best night ever."

This explanation brought sentimental tears to Georgia's eyes. "Well, then I am more glad than ever that I am here with you. Now you must tell me which of the gentlemen you most enjoyed this evening. I want to be sure to take note of who you might be married to after I leave."

Vicky giggled and threw herself onto the bed. "I cannot say that any one particular gentleman has captured my heart as of yet. I just really enjoyed feeling popular for once."

"Come on Vick, some of them must be more interesting than others."

"Well, it really matters very little because I doubt I can marry before we get Rosabel and Hilaria committed."

Georgia laughed. "Committed? Like in Bedlam? Perhaps it would do them some good."

The two went off into gales of laughter before subsiding into a comfortable gossip session as the maids helped them get ready for bed.

"Oh, good heavens!" Vicky declared. "I never asked what you and the earl talked about over supper."

Georgia's yawn wasn't fake, but she was happy that it overtook her at that moment. It added to the air of nonchalance she was hoping to cultivate. "Oh, not much of interest. He is becoming tedious with his apologies. There is nothing that can be done to change what happened, so I really do wish he would cease."

"Is that all? It seemed as though you were both quite engrossed." Despite her sleepiness, Vicky's gaze seemed searching.

Georgia shrugged. "He did say he'd like to take me for another ride to add to my enjoyment of my stay here in London, so he's to collect me at four o'clock this afternoon."

"And you agreed? You said it was dull the first time."

"He said he would take me to Gunther's," she answered with a laugh. "How could I refuse?"

"Did you get me invited along, too?" Vicky wondered with a giggle.

"I rather thought with how popular you were tonight that you would have invitations of your own."

"We shall see," Vicky replied, trying to remain mysterious. "We are both going to be ladies about Town this week."

"I quite like the sound of that," Georgia concluded with a chuckle before drifting off to sleep.

Chapter Twelve

Despite reassuring herself she wasn't really looking forward to spending any time with the earl, the day seemed to drag as Georgia waited for Lord Crossley to arrive. After their late night, it had been nearly noon by the time she and Vicky had gotten up and broken their fast. Then there was the luxurious time having their hair done. That was the one thing Georgia would miss most about her time in London. In the village she had always, and would forevermore continue, to style her own hair every day. She was not nearly as skilled as the Sherton maids. Her sigh as she gazed into the mirror was heartfelt.

"What was that about?" Vicky asked with a grin.

"My hair," Georgia replied with an answering grin. "It is the utmost decadence having someone to brush and arrange it for me. I shall miss it when I go home."

"I thought we agreed not to discuss you leaving."

"Of course," Georgia agreed with a smile. "What shall we do with ourselves until we go to the Park?"

"We could make some calls or do some shopping. I would like to stop in at the lending library."

"Whatever for? It is not as though you will have any time to read."

"One can always make time for books, Georgia," Vicky scolded with a giggle. "Especially if you insist upon leaving me."

"Well, then you shan't need any for a while yet." She paused for a moment before continuing with a cajoling tone. "What would you say to going for a walk so I can explore the neighbourhood?"

"Oh Georgie, I completely forgot how much you wanted to explore. But can't you see the neighbourhood while we drive around?"

"It is not at all the same," Georgia explained. "For one thing, depending on the conveyance, you can't always see very much. Or one must pay attention to the driver. Or speed is a factor." Her voice was momentarily muffled as the maid passed her gown over her head. "Besides, you could look at it as an adventure, since it seems to me as though you probably have never actually walked around your neighbourhood."

Vicky couldn't deny her friend's words and acquiesced with a laugh. "Very well, but we shall require a maid or footman to accompany us or my mother will not allow it."

This had not occurred to Georgia, and she bit her lip in indecision as she turned to the maids. One quickly bobbed a curtsy.

"Do not worry your head about us, Miss Georgia, any one of us would be happy to come with you. It's not often we get a chance to go for a walk, and most of us would probably enjoy it as much as you."

Georgia smiled her gratitude at the maid and turned back to Vicky with a grin, wiggling her eyebrows. "See?"

With a good-natured huff, Vicky agreed. "Very well. It's a good thing we are dressed appropriately so we needn't waste any time changing. Would you like to leave straight away?"

"I would love to, thank you for asking."

Both girls dissolved into laughter as they set off from the room. After leaving a message with the footman to pass along to Lady Sherton, they were soon striding down the street.

"Mind you, we aren't in the country Georgie, we needn't hurry anywhere. We need to conserve our energy for dancing later."

Georgia rolled her eyes. "You sound like an old maid."

Vicky stopped in her tracks. "How could you say something so hurtful?"

Georgia was about to offer profuse apologies when she noticed the twinkle shining in her friend's eyes. It appeared that Vicky's efforts to keep a serious expression on her face were failing and she soon dissolved into giggles.

When she regained her control, they continued their stroll. There was still laughter in her voice when Vicky had to admit, "You are quite right, I did sound deadly dull, didn't I? But it is not at all the thing to be seen bounding about the city. And if you will recall, it was our last walk about Town that got you into your troubles with Lord Crossley in the first place."

"Are you trying to say that it is my fault?" Georgia gasped. "You are the one who misspoke to him."

Vicky waved her hand through the air as though brushing the words away. "Of course not, my dear, do not be a goose. I was merely trying to illustrate that young ladies of the *ton* do not make a habit of exerting themselves while in Town."

Georgia gazed at her friend, trying to discern whether or not she was now being serious. Vicky gazed back at her before a grin spread across her face. "I do realize that I sound silly, but it is how things are in London." She paused for a moment before sighing. "This is exactly why I needed you to come with me. Do keep me from turning into a total simpleton, I beg of you."

Georgia tucked her hand through her friend's elbow and squeezed her arm. "You are far from being a simpleton, have no fear. Now come along and tell me what you know about this street. I love the architecture here. Were you around when they were being built?"

Vigilia smiled at her companion but shook her head. "No, I think this block was constructed about ten years ago. When we were all little my mother wouldn't countenance travelling to London with us in tow. She herself didn't come very often or for very long, but I almost never set foot in the city before I was fifteen. But my father talked about it a little bit, if I recall. He was admiring how modern the finishes were inside, but he had hated the smoke produced by the kilns as they made the bricks."

"They made the bricks right here on the spot?"

"Apparently that is the usual way of it. Father says the soil is particularly good for bricks and it saves having to get rid of the dirt when they dig the cellars and so on."

"How fascinating that would be to see."

"You are an odd creature, Georgia Holton, but I love you anyway."

The two girls grinned as they continued their walk.

Finally, when Georgia could no longer convince Vicky to continue, they returned home to prepare for their drives.

"Did you tell me who you are going driving with, Vicky? I apologize, but at the moment I cannot recall."

"No, I didn't tell you because I wasn't sure at the time we were talking about it. But Lord Cheltenham sent me some flowers this morning with a note asking if I would ride with him."

"Lord Cheltenham?" Georgia repeated with a question mark evident in her tone. "Is he the handsome baron who was wearing the teal waistcoat?"

"No, that was Lord Farnsworth. Lord Cheltenham is a viscount. He is quite tall with wavy chestnut hair. He likes to talk about his horses."

Georgia laughs. "Don't all the gentlemen? That hardly narrows it down. But I do think I recall meeting your viscount. He seemed pleasant. Is there something particularly noteworthy about Lord Cheltenham that caused you to accept his invitation?"

"Do you mean besides the fact that he extended it?" Vicky's laugh sounded a trifle forced, causing Georgia to turn to her with concern. "Oh don't look like that, my dear, I am not about to turn into a watering pot. It is just that I have never felt successful during my time amongst Society, following after my sisters last year. Having you here seems to be making all the difference."

"Perhaps having me around is setting you at ease and making it more comfortable to converse with the gentlemen," Georgia surmised.

"Whatever the case, it is lovely. But in further answer to your question, Lord Cheltenham was one of the few gentlemen with whom I spoke during previous Seasons. While I still don't know him very well, and this is the first time he has asked me to go driving, there is something appealing about him that I cannot quite put into words."

"Are you comfortable around him?"

"Of all the gentlemen I've met, I am the least tongue-tied with him," Vicky answered with a giggle.

"Well then that is a definite mark in his favour," Georgia declared with alacrity. "Tell me more about this viscount. Is he someone's heir and that is just a courtesy title, or has he already lost his father?"

"He inherited from his grandfather just last year. He lost his father when he was a boy."

"Then he is no doubt considered to be quite the catch, I would imagine. How has he managed to keep the match-making mamas at bay?"

Vicky shrugged. "His estates are not the most lucrative, it would seem, but I believe he is comfortably situated. He wasn't about in Society much for a time as he was in mourning. I suspect he might be paying me some attention because I'm safe from him with my older sisters still single."

"But would it really be so terrible if you were to marry before Hil or Bel? Why are you so determined that you cannot marry until after they do?"

"Well, Georgia, it just isn't done, for one thing. For another, I think it would hurt their feelings. Do you know, Hil has never even received a single offer?"

Georgia's face must have displayed her lack of shock over this because Vicky laughed and continued. "Yes, I know, that isn't the most shocking piece of news, but what IS shocking is that Rosabel hasn't received nearly as many offers as one might expect." She paused again. "Of course, I haven't received anything approaching an offer, but if I did, it might be incredibly hurtful to my sisters, especially Hilaria. So in my mind, it is impossible to accept an offer before they have."

Georgia was silent for a moment while she digested her friend's words. "You are the kindest girl I know. No wonder you are my best friend. Your sisters don't even realize how lovely you are, do they?"

Vicky blushed and shrugged. "It might be a sister thing. I believe they would do it for me if the roles were reversed."

"Do you really?" Georgia was dubious but had no desire to hurt her friend, so she quickly moved on. "I would give my life for any one of my siblings, but I thought that was because I'm the oldest and practically their mother. You give me hope that the feelings might be reciprocated even on some level. I would never expect the level of sacrifice you are making from them, but they are still children so the point is moot."

The young ladies continued their stroll in quiet contemplation for a couple moments. They were almost back to the Sherton townhouse when Georgia spoke up. "I still think you should give Lord Cheltenham a chance. If you truly develop feelings for him, your sisters will not begrudge your happiness. Considering how you feel about the Season, you shouldn't put yourself through this endlessly."

"Mayhap I shall prevail upon you to join me again next year," Vicky pronounced with a grin. "It is neither a trial nor dull while you are here."

Georgia smiled gently before reminding her friend. "I shall have to be making arrangements of my own once I return to the village, Vick, you know that. I need to ensure more stability for the children than my father seems capable of providing."

Vicky sighed. "Well, never mind about all these maudlin thoughts. Let us have a lovely afternoon before we dance a hole in our slippers this evening."

"That sounds utterly decadent. Lead on."

By the time they arrived back home there was just barely enough time to run up to their room and have the maid tidy their hair before Crossley was due to arrive.

"Are you sure you don't mind me going out before you?" Georgia worried.

"Not at all. I told you I would want to make time for some reading. This will be the perfect opportunity."

Vicky was sitting at the window watching for the earl's arrival. "Is that a child sitting beside Crossley?" She was incredulous.

Georgia bit her lip and hoped she did not betray herself with her blush. She had avoided telling her best friend the most salient part of her conversation with the earl. Vicky's shrewd eyes skewered her. "This is why he is coming at such an early hour, isn't it? You sly thing. You have some explaining to do when you get back here."

Georgia had to laugh at her friend's reaction. "Hopefully, I will have an explanation to offer," she replied with a shrug before running to give Vicky a quick hug when they heard the knocker echo through the house. "You try to have fun with Cheltenham!" she admonished firmly. "Take mental notes so you can tell me all about it when we are back together."

"I do not think I am the one that will have the most interesting tales. I tell you the same, you absolutely *must* tell me all when you get back here."

Georgia didn't make any promises, merely blew a kiss and left the room. She wouldn't have been able to explain in that moment why she was so reluctant to promise, only being quite certain that the earl's secrets were hiding deep inner scars and while she fully trusted Vicky, she would never want to open the man up to public scrutiny nor ridicule.

When she got to the bottom of the stairs, he was standing by the door, his stiff posture revealing his discomfort. Georgia felt a moment of regret that she had forced the situation upon him, but she swallowed it. It was for his own good and that of the poor boy waiting in his carriage. He seemed to rid himself of his brooding when he caught sight of her. What appeared to be a genuine smile spread across his face.

He bowed to her. "I appreciate your punctuality, Miss Holton. Might I be permitted to say you look lovely today?"

She offered him a curtsy. "No young woman would deny anyone the opportunity to say such a thing, thank you, my lord," she replied with a grin as she rose from the respectful stance.

"I don't suppose you want to keep your horses waiting, so we ought to be off," she added when he didn't appear in any hurry to take his leave. *He really ought to overcome his reluctance to be in that poor child's presence*, she thought with a grimace she tried to hide.

No doubt he perceived her intentions for he regarded her with shrewd eyes and a crooked smile. "Of course not, the poor horses shan't know what to do with themselves if left on the street," was all he said as the butler opened the door for them.

Georgia tried to ignore how many windows of the house had faces pressed to them, watching as she descended the front stairs on the arm of the Earl of Crossley. When her gaze encountered the pale face of the boy sitting perfectly still in the corner of the barouche, her heart melted and all other thoughts fled from her mind.

"Hello, young sir, you must be Master Christopher." She didn't bother with whatever courtesy title the child might carry. It was enough that she knew his name.

The look of surprise on his face caused her stomach to clench and her heart to harden further against the earl, but she kept her smile pleasant and her focus on the boy. When he nodded shyly she continued to offer an encouraging smile while she introduced herself. "My name is Georgia Holton. It is a pleasure to make your acquaintance." She held out her hand for him to shake.

The small boy glanced nervously at the earl but reached out to shake her hand despite his obvious fear. He then delighted her with his perceptive question. "Were you named after the king?"

She grinned at him. "I was. How did you guess?"

He shrugged. "There are a lot of Georges, and my nurse talks about it a lot."

Georgia laughed. "My parents were terribly patriotic when I was born. It is a little bit embarrassing, but while I too know many Georges, I haven't yet met another Georgia, so I am impressed that you figured it out." She kept her attention on the boy, not particularly caring about the earl's reaction. "Do you like your nurse?"

Christopher looked surprised by the question, as though he had never pondered the thought. He offered her a lopsided shrug, much like one she had seen the earl offer before. "She can be very strict but she is all I've got, really, so I s'pose I do like her. She says she ain't raising no mamby pamby boy so she won't be coddling me, but she gives very nice hugs if I ever have nightmares."

Georgia's heart was won by the youngster in that moment. "She sounds quite sensible to me. I think I would like her, too. Does she ever give you sweets?"

The boy looked sideways at the earl, making Georgia laugh. "I probably shouldn't have asked you such a personal question. I beg your forgiveness. Never mind that question. Have you started taking lessons yet?"

Christopher looked grateful at her change of subject and seemed quite keen to discuss his lessons, launching into a description of all that he had already learned. After a few moments, Georgia laughed. "I am quite impressed. You must have started your lessons very early if you have learned so much already. Or you might be particularly brilliant." His little chest puffed up over her words, causing her to want to laugh but she struggled not to burst the child's fragile sensitivities.

By then they had arrived in the Park, which was virtually deserted in comparison to the last time she had been there with the earl. But Georgia barely noticed, so engrossed was she with the small boy. When she finally realized where they were, she grinned at him. "Are you familiar with this park, Christopher?"

He again glanced nervously at the earl, but she was glad to see he was growing less uncomfortable and quickly nodded in reply to her question.

"Do you have a favourite spot?"

His nod was more enthusiastic now. "Feeding the ducks on the river."

"Oh that does sound delightful, but I didn't think to bring any crumbs." Both she and the boy turned to look at the earl.

"Don't look at me. I don't have any bread either," he grumbled but didn't look nearly as tense as he had when he had handed her into the carriage.

"Perhaps the ducks won't be too upset with us if we stop by to have a look at them even with empty hands. We shall just apologize to them and promise to bring twice as much next time we come. Can you show me where they are?"

The youngster was gazing at Georgia with adoration, clearly enjoying the adult attention from someone other than the servants. His vigorous nod nearly shook the barouche, and Georgia's clear laugh rang out. Christopher pointed in the appropriate direction and with a subtle exchange between the earl and the driver they set off to find the ducks.

~~~

Crispin was feeling decidedly unnerved. Surprisingly, he was enjoying the presence of the boy and was fascinated with the young woman beside him. Her interested questions were drawing out the child in a way that he had never witnessed, and his answers were showing the boy to be an intelligent, polite youngster. One that any man should be proud to lay claim to. As Georgia had pointed out, whether he was truly his son or not, the boy was his heir, and he really ought to take a hand in
~~~

raising him. Crispin wanted to resent her interference in his life but was feeling strangely relaxed in both their presence. What he did find himself resenting was Georgia's obvious preference for the child over himself. Crispin would never have thought himself capable of being jealous of a five-year-old, but here he was watching the byplay between Miss Holton and young Christopher and wishing he could somehow be a part of it.

When his driver pulled the barouche to a standstill off to the side of the road, under a large tree, he quickly stepped down and turned to help the other occupants. The boy politely waited while Miss Holton stood, took Crispin's hand and quickly alighted. Turning to Christopher, Crispin found himself holding his breath to see how the boy would react to his offer of help. When they had climbed silently into the barouche before leaving to collect Miss Holton, the boy had done so without assistance, avoiding any unnecessary contact with the foreboding earl glowering at his side. Now, despite his nervous glances, he was smiling eagerly, and Crispin found it endearing. He hated to admit that Miss Holton was right, but it really wasn't the boy's fault whatever his mother might have done. Crispin resolved to do better in future for the youngster.

But Georgia could obviously not read his mind. Having no idea of his change of heart, she continued to ignore him in favour of the boy, and the two held hands, walking ahead of him toward the water. Crispin trailed in their wake.

The two in front of him appeared to be enraptured with the ducks that were quacking rather urgently at them. They were sorely disappointed when the birds swam away after realizing their spectators had empty hands. Crispin felt like laughing over their equally dejected faces. Despite her obvious maturity, Miss Holton could be almost childlike at times. He was reminded that the chit was really barely out of the schoolroom despite her almost mother-like air at times. He was swept with the urge to protect them both.

His stomach clenched when he realized the direction of his thoughts. He quickly shoved the unwelcome thoughts away. While he would do better for the child in the future, he had absolutely no desire to become attached to another woman. He had his heir. He had no need for another despite the usual expectation of having a spare. Women were not to be trusted, he reminded himself once again.

"I think you are getting much too close to the edge, both of you. Since your feathered friends are apparently too fickle, what say you to a trip to Gunther's?"

Georgia's eyes lit up, but the boy merely looked confused. "What's Gunther's?" he asked, turning to Georgia.

She threw a glare at Crispin quickly before bending down to answer the boy's question. "Gunther's is the most delightful place. I have not yet had the pleasure of visiting there yet, either, but I have heard they have every sweet you could ever have imagined. My mouth nearly waters just at the thought of it. We shan't know what to choose, I am sure of it."

The boy looked puzzled still but was enraptured with Miss Holton, so he followed her lead and turned away from the river without further argument.

Crispin had to bite the inside of his cheek to prevent laughter when he watched Georgia trying to divide herself between glaring at him for his negligence toward the child while still smiling encouragingly at the boy.

"What is your favourite kind of dessert, Cristopher?"

"I don't eat dessert." The boy's soft reply was followed by a brief but heavy silence.

"Do you not have a sweet tooth?"

"I don't really know what that means, Miss, but I am not allowed to eat sweets. I'm not sure if I should come with you to this Gunther's place."

The look of bewilderment on Georgia's face made Crispin again want to comfort her. However, he resisted the urge to put his arm around her with some effort.

"Who told you that you aren't allowed? I am most certain the earl here is responsible for you, so if he offers to take you somewhere, you can be sure that you are allowed to go."

The serious little boy thought this through for a moment. "My governess says sweets will rot my teeth and the earl will never like me if I have no teeth." He whispered the words to Georgia while darting his gaze toward the earl.

Crispin didn't feel so much like laughing anymore. He could see how his churlish behavior toward the boy was damaging to him. Hopefully the situation was not irredeemable. He hesitated, trying to think of something to say to ease the awkward situation. He needn't have worried. With Miss Holton present, awkward situations didn't stand a chance.

"Do you not clean your teeth every night before you go to bed?"

"Of course I do, Miss. I never forget. I'm a big boy now." His little chest puffed up with these words.

"Well then, I don't think you have anything to worry about. As long as you spend a little extra time tonight on your teeth you should be perfectly fine." She paused for a moment before leaning forward and whispering to the boy. "I shan't tell your governess and as long as you look after your teeth, she need not ever know."

Christopher's wide gaze examined Georgia's face to gauge her sincerity. Seemingly satisfied with whatever he saw there, he then turned his serious face toward the earl and spoke to him directly for the first time. "Are you truly going to give me sweets, my lord?"

"I truly am."

The boy broke out into a grin. It transformed his face. Crispin's stomach turned over when he realized how very much the youngster resembled his late wife. He turned his gaze to the passing scenery. Miss Holton quickly took over the conversation.

"Now Christopher, I do have to add, though, that while we are going to keep this little secret from your governess, it is only an exception because you are with the earl. In the usual run of things, you do have to listen to whatever guidance your governess gives you. Do you agree?"

The boy's serious gaze was back focused on her. "I suppose so."

"The earl is your guardian, so he has the final say in all matters. If he is not present, he has delegated that authority to her. Does that make sense to you?"

Christopher nodded but then asked, "For how long?"

"Do you mean, how long do you have to obey the governess?"

The boy shrugged. "How long do I have to *have* a governess?"

"That you will have to take up with the earl. Perhaps you will eventually get a tutor or go to school, so you probably won't always have a governess. But you will always have to listen to the earl or whoever he designates until you are all grown up."

He kept his intense focus on her face, not even flickering a glance toward the earl. "But *why*?"

"Why do you have to do as the earl says?"

He offered a lopsided shrug. "Why is he my guardian?"

No laughter lurked anywhere in his soul now as Crispin watched the two other occupants of the barouche. He watched Georgia struggle to come up with an answer to the boy's question. She swallowed down the tears that welled in her eyes briefly. Her hesitation was momentary and if he hadn't been watching her so closely, he would have missed the emotions that flitted across her features. She quickly recovered, flicked a glance toward him, and then offered the boy a wide smile.

"Because you are just that lucky, my young friend. If not for the earl being your guardian, you would not be sitting in this fine barouche on this lovely day heading toward the most delicious treats your mouth has ever experienced."

The boy blinked for a moment, looked at the earl, and then brought his gaze back to Georgia's animated face. His answering grin caused Crispin to release the breath he hadn't even realized he had been holding.

The rest of the afternoon passed in a blur. His two companions dithered over their selections, unable to decide on just one dessert, before finally agreeing to order two different things and sharing both. He was shocked to find that he enjoyed watching their excitement. If anyone had previously told him that taking a chit and a child to Gunther's could be a good time, he would have told them they were in their cups. But he here was, stone cold sober, and delighting in the simple pleasure of giving someone else joy.

Crispin rather thought he had never actively contributed toward another person's joy before. It was a singular experience. One he would like to have again, he realized with a little bit of awkwardness. He barely tasted his own treat. He hadn't much cared what he ordered, more interested in watching his companions. When they finished their own desserts and then eyed his, he couldn't help his laughter as he slid his plate toward them.

"Have at it. I am quite content with my coffee."

They both wore guilty expressions but didn't wait for him to take back his offer. They made quick work of finishing off the last of the sweets.

With a sinking feeling, Crispin realized it was time to return Miss Holton to her home. He wished the afternoon could stretch on into eternity but shook his head at that ridiculous thought. He tried to summon his usual reminder that women were not to be trusted but couldn't muster much enthusiasm for the sentiment. Christopher had certainly grown attached to her quickly, and the earl didn't think the boy trusted anyone. Crispin had the sneaking suspicion that he had already given the girl his trust. He certainly had never introduced his heir to anyone else of his acquaintance before. He barely acknowledged the boy's existence with anyone else, yet here he was spending time with the two least likely people he had ever encountered. And enjoying himself. It was a fact to cause marvel.

"Well, this has been the best afternoon I've yet had since coming to London," Miss Holton was saying, her warm attention focused on the child. "I dearly enjoyed making your acquaintance, Christopher. Thank you for sharing my first taste of Gunther's with me."

The boy's grin stretched around only a little bit of chocolate. With a chuckle, Miss Holton grabbed a napkin and wiped his face quickly. He didn't even have a chance to protest before it was over. She leaned in and excused her behaviour. "It would not do to have your governess see the evidence, now would it?"

They shared another grin before the chit stood and once again proved that she had very little use of him. "My lord, it has been a pleasure, but I truly must be getting home. Ought I to walk from here?"

Crispin felt the heat climbing into his cheeks. *As though I would allow her to walk*, he thought with indignation. "Of course not, Miss Holton. We will see you home."

"Very well, but if it is not too inconvenient, it would be best if we make haste, as the hour is advancing."

He had to laugh over her managing ways.

Georgia and Christopher chattered away as the earl sat quietly observing. He would never have thought the boy would display to advantage, but in Miss Holton's company he had blossomed into a becoming child. Crispin determined to ensure he spent more time in the child's company in the future.

When he was handing Georgia down from the carriage, he had tried to get her to commit to saving him a dance later that evening, but she refused to make any promises. "We shall see, my lord. If you end up in the same ballroom as me this evening and I have any room left on my dance card, I will consider placing your name there," was all she would allow.

He sat in the barouche and watched as she went up the stairs and into the house with an elegant, light step. When he straightened around, he was surprised to find himself caught by the youngster's serious stare.

"Will we ever see her again, my lord?"

"I sincerely hope so." Crispin gave the boy the truth.

The boy sighed. "Me, too. Everything is better with her around, isn't it?"

Crispin was afraid the boy might be right but didn't bother answering him. They rode in silence for a couple minutes.

"Thank you for the treats today, my lord. Henny said I wasn't to get my expectations riled up that you would want to spend time with me another day, but thank you for today anyway."

The earl was humbled by the child's mature words but angered by the embarrassing truth in them. He rather thought the boy might be in need of a new governess.

"You are quite welcome, Christopher. It was far more enjoyable than I expected as well."

They were quiet for another brief space while Crispin thought despairingly that he had no idea what to discuss with the boy. He hadn't paid that close attention when Georgia was talking to him; he had been absorbing the experience rather than taking in the details.

"Do you like your governess, Christopher?"

The boy shrugged. "Not particularly. Your cook is much nicer than my governess. Nurse is nice, but Henny says I'll soon be too old to keep her. And the maids and footmen are pretty nice, too. They let me follow them around if I can get away from Henny. It's more interesting when we're in the country because the grooms there let me help them with the horses. Here, the grooms won't let me even look at the horses."

Crispin blinked, surprised that he had volunteered so much information. "Well, my horses could be dangerous."

"I know. I'm pretty sure that's how my mother died." He didn't seem particularly troubled by that fact, but Crispin felt horrified by the child's words.

"What do you know about it?"

"Not much." Now the boy looked as though he were about to shrink back into the silent shell he had been in before the transforming presence of Miss Holton.

"You needn't be afraid of talking to me, Christopher," Crispin felt compelled to say, hoping to reassure the child. Georgia had been right after all. Whatever had gone on between the earl and his late wife was not this child's fault. Legally, the boy was his son. It was possible he was, in fact. But since Crispin was well aware that his wife had been incapable of fidelity, he had always questioned the boy's paternity. Now he saw that it didn't matter. The boy was his heir. He deserved to be treated as the cherished son of the House of Crossley.

Feeling as though a load had been lifted off his chest, Crispin felt a bubble of gratitude welling up from within him toward Miss Holton. He was all the more indebted to her. The earl resolved to dance with her that night and tell her so.

Chapter Thirteen

Georgia was relieved to learn from the footman that Vicky had not yet returned. She ran up to their shared room, shut the door quietly behind her, and then sank down to the floor in a heap of petticoats. She was exhausted. Her emotions felt as though they had been trampled on by his lordship's large horses.

She had felt every feeling she could possibly name. Her heart went out to the small boy. His quiet acceptance of his unfortunate circumstances made her want to weep. And the earl's treatment of the child made her want to become violent. But the earl's kindness that afternoon, his patience while she and Christopher had such trouble deciding what to order, and his handsome face, and warm chuckle, had made it particularly difficult to hold onto her anger with him. When she wasn't fighting the urge to hit him, she had to fight the opposing urge to throw herself into his arms and tell him she could help him make it all better.

But that was ridiculous. What could she possibly know about helping the earl make his life better? She was a provincial girl from a small village. Barely acceptable socially in the circles he ran with. Besides, what could she offer the earl? She was barely twenty years old and had a promised dowry of ten pounds. A small fortune to her, a life changing amount. But it would probably barely keep the earl supplied with snuff for a month. In addition, she had her young brothers and sisters to think about. If the earl couldn't be trusted with one child, she couldn't entrust him with four more. No, she thought, it was merely the joy of being with a child again that turned her head. *And I must not have slept soundly last night. I am merely tired.*

She pulled herself back to her feet and gave serious thought to taking a nap, but then she heard what must be Vicky's rapid approach to their room. Plastering on what she hoped was a carefree smile, Georgia braced herself for the upcoming conversation.

"Vicky," she greeted with mustered enthusiasm. "How was your outing with Cheltenham? Do the roses in your cheeks mean you had a good time?"

"Yes, yes, it was delightful, or it would have been had I not been consumed with curiosity as to how *your* afternoon was proceeding."

"Oh no, I pray you, tell me you are jesting with me." Georgia's already overwrought emotions couldn't handle guilt to be piled on top of the writhing heap.

Her distress must have been written on her face as Vicky quickly reassured her. "Of course, I'm teasing you, silly. Cheltenham was a delight and the afternoon flew by, but you cannot think for a single moment that I forgot my questions about your afternoon. Now, you really must confess all. I shan't give you a single moment of peace until I am sure you have divulged all that you have clearly been keeping from me."

Georgia had to giggle over Vicky's words, thus setting them both at ease. "Very well, I had no intention of keeping anything from you. I just didn't really know the facts myself. They still aren't all that clear to me, I must admit, but I will tell you whatever I can. But do not let my capitulation make you think that you can avoid telling me about Cheltenham."

Both girls grinned at each other while Georgia continued. "The boy you saw is the earl's heir. When I went for a ride with Crossley previously, we saw the child with his governess, that is how I was aware of his existence. When the earl insisted that he wanted to do something for me to make up for saying too much about me to Lord Layton, I told him he could make it up to me by introducing me to the child. I explained that I was missing my brothers and sisters so much that spending time with a youngster would make me feel better."

"And he fell for that yarn?"

Georgia grinned. "Apparently so. It wasn't completely untrue."

Vicky rolled her eyes. "It has only been a few days since you saw them. I am quite certain you could survive several more without going into a decline."

"Well never mind that, the earl agreed, and the boy really was a delight. His name is Christopher and he is five years old. He's been well brought up despite the earl's neglect but clearly thirsts for attention."

"You were meddling, weren't you?" Vicky shrewdly observed. Georgia felt heat climbing into her cheeks and merely offered a shrug.

"Someone had to do something. It was for both their good."

Vicky laughed. "Do you think it worked?"

Georgia shrugged. "Only time will tell, I suppose. I do think Crossley was able to see that Christopher is an innocent child who deserves to be treated well. What he does with that information is really hard to tell. The man likes to consider himself an enigma. And I don't know him nearly well enough to be able to read him." She sighed.

"That seemed heartfelt," Vicky said.

"What did?"

"Your sigh. Do you wish you could read him better?" Now Vicky's tone had turned sly.

Georgia felt heat climbing into her cheeks once more. "I beg you, do not go reading anything into my interaction with the earl. He is not for me, even if I were in search of an aristocratic husband. Which I'm not. He is far too suspicious. And dark. I do not think I could live with someone who prefers looking at the negative side of things at all times."

"Perhaps you could show him the error of his ways."

Georgia laughed and threw a pillow at her friend. "Now enough about Crossley, I want to know more about your afternoon. Do tell me you were merely jesting earlier."

"I already told you that I was, you ninny. Now, I will tell you all about it while the maid is doing our hair. If we are going to continue to be the belles of the ball, we must put some effort into it, or everyone will consider we were merely lucky the last time."

Georgia rolled her eyes and threw another pillow at her but dutifully followed Vicky's directions as a maid hurried into the room in response to Vicky's vigorous tug on the bell.

"We are both going to strain your skills today, Margaret, so thank you for coming quickly. We want the most intricate styles you can muster."

Far from daunting the maid, Georgia was surprised to see the girl looked pleased by Vicky's declaration. She clapped her hands and grinned.

"I'll be right pleased to tie your hair right up, my lady. Which one of you wants to get started first?"

Georgia grinned at her hostess. "This was your idea, my dear. You ought to be the first one to enjoy Margaret's ministrations."

Vicky didn't argue, quickly getting settled in front of the mirror.

"Cheltenham is a pleasant enough fellow, not nearly as complicated as your afternoon's companion. I now know that his stables contain at least ten horses. If I thought hard enough on the subject, I could probably even recite for you their names and maybe even their sizes."

"Good heavens, really? Is that all the gentleman spoke of?"

"Pretty much."

"Then why did you seem so delighted when you returned?"

Vicky laughed. "Because, unlike you, I like simple. Your background makes you more open to complicated."

Georgia joined her friend's laughter. "I suppose so. I've been managing a household for years and juggling the children and everything else. I'm used to it," she concluded with a shrug.

"Which is why Crossley might be the perfect match for you," Vicky persisted.

Georgia laughed again but shook her head at her friend. "I don't actually think the earl is on the Marriage Mart, despite his attendance at balls and routs. He is still angry with his dead wife. It seems to have scarred him. And yes, his knowledge of our little situation with my inheritance makes him the only possible match in Town, but I still think I'll be much better off returning to Sherton and getting the smithy or the baker to marry me."

Vicky looked sceptical. "You just want someone you can boss around, and you're afraid an earl won't let you."

Georgia grinned but firmly answered. "I can assure you, Vick, the earl isn't pursuing me so this is a moot point. Now tell me some more about the event we're attending tonight so I can be a little more prepared for who I shall meet."

Thus successfully diverting her friend, the conversation continued to flow and they chattered their way down to the foyer to await the rest of the family.

Chapter Fourteen

Lady Sherton had insisted they could not be the first to arrive. Her edict was obeyed. The rooms were already quite full by the time their entourage arrived in the ballroom. Rosabel and Hilaria each had their own groups of friends that soon absorbed them into the crowd. Lady Sherton admonished the girls to behave before she too went her own way.

Georgia and Vicky exchanged amused glances before directing their attention to the crowds. They were soon surrounded by acquaintances. Before long, Georgia found herself on the dance floor. She began to feel that thousands of eyes were following her progress. She tried to ignore the sensation, reasoning that she was merely unused to such crowds. But then her partner commented on it.

"I say, Miss Holton, I do hope I am not doing anything untoward. Does it not feel to you as though everyone were watching us?"

Georgia laughed. "I thought I was imagining it, but you are right, it does feel as though everyone's eyes are following us. I don't think we're doing anything particularly out of the ordinary."

The gentleman in whose arms she was circling the floor grinned at her. "I have never found myself to be the centre of attention before. I am certain we ought to do something to take advantage of the situation."

Georgia wasn't sure if she liked the direction his thoughts were going, but she offered him a valiant smile in return. "What did you have in mind, my lord?"

She must not have hidden her trepidation successfully as he returned her smile. "No need to fear, my lady, I shan't shame you in any way. But I do think we ought to make it worth their effort of watching us." With those words, he spun her in a sudden dramatic circle.

Thankfully, she was quick on her feet and managed not to fall on her face. She had no idea the gentleman had such a dramatic flair, but she soon lost count of the number of spins and dips he performed with her in his arms. Georgia couldn't decide if she was enjoying it or not. She wasn't disappointed when the dance came to an end.

Bowing over her hand, the gentleman offered her another grin. "That was delightful, Miss Holton, thank you for the dance. Shall I escort you to the refreshment room for a glass of punch?"

She was just about to accept when she caught sight of Vicky trying to beckon her frantically but discretely. It was such a humorously contradictory display that she had to struggle not to burst into laughter. "Thank you, my lord, but I think I must rejoin my friends," she managed to stammer out.

She went across the room as quickly as propriety would allow. "What is going on?" she demanded when she reached Vicky, who was huddled together with her sister Hilaria. "You both look as though you are about to burst and I'm not sure if it is with anger or laughter."

"Did you notice that every eye in the room was following you just now?"

"Yes, Hilaria, but I couldn't control what his lordship was doing. Your mother was most explicit that the gentleman must always be the one to take the lead in the dance."

She could hear Vicky stifling laughter, but Georgia managed to keep a straight face and her eyes on Hilaria.

"Now is not the time to make jokes. Everyone is talking about you. They are saying you are a renowned heiress and half the fortune hunters in the room are queuing up for you as we speak."

Georgia blinked and had to exert considerable effort not to crane around to see how literally she ought to take Hilaria's words. She wondered why the other woman would care even if it were true. She wasn't left to wonder for long.

"If you cause a scandal, it will ruin all our chances," she hissed. "How did you manage to make such a mull of things?"

"I do not see how you have managed to come to the conclusion that this is all my fault." Georgia went on the defensive.

"You can be certain no one in our family said any such thing about you. In fact, I am most certain Mama has been at great pains to ensure it be known that your circumstances are less than ideal, if anyone went to the effort of asking. You were supposed to just be here to keep Vicky out of trouble. Instead you've stirred up a mess. We never should have allowed you to come." Hilaria stamped her foot and flounced away, leaving Vicky and Georgia staring in her wake.

"Do you have any idea what she was talking about?" Georgia asked, while still watching Hilaria's dark head bobbing through the crowd.

"It does seem as though you are generating more than the usual attention this evening. I think people are talking about you even more than they were before."

Georgia glanced around the room, her enjoyment of the evening drooping as she saw the number of fans held up in front of whispering mouths as eyes watched her avidly. The small orchestra was just starting up the next dance, and she determined to use the opportunity to slip from the room.

"Could I have the pleasure of this dance, Miss Holton?"

A shiver ran down her spine as she recognized the deep tones of the Earl of Crossley. She wished the floor would open and swallow her.

"Now is not the best time, my lord. I was just about to…"

He cut her off midsentence. "You are not going anywhere, my girl. Now is not the time for retreat. Hold your head high and ignore the gossip. Dance with me."

Georgia cast Vicky a bewildered glance before being whisked onto the dance floor. Just her luck, it was a waltz. She wasn't as familiar with the steps as with the country dances. And she could not escape the earl for even a moment, as there would be no separating during this dance. She offered him a wan smile.

"What do you know of the situation, my lord?"

"I know I'm much to blame for your current predicament. And I know what it's like to be the centre of unwanted attention. Can you imagine what it was like for me when my wife died under a cloud of suspicion?"

"I can't even imagine, my lord, but what has that to do with me?"

"I had to stand alone and face the scandal. I cannot stand by and watch you do the same, not when I'm at fault."

"This really isn't your business, my lord. And I would happily just leave Town and return home, but Lady Hilaria just informed me that this is somehow going to taint her and her sisters." Georgia felt tears well in her eyes for a moment but was distracted from her distress when the earl tightened his grip on her and another thrill shivered up her spine.

"You cannot run away from your troubles. That will never solve anything."

"But there is nothing that can be done to fix this. Perhaps if I am gone, it will slip from everyone's minds just as quickly as it arrived. I am easily forgettable, I am sure."

"I doubt that," Crossley murmured near her ear.

Georgia shivered. She still hadn't looked fully into the earl's face; she was a little nervous of what she would see there. Steeling her nerves, she glanced up and nearly faltered in her steps. The earl was gazing at her with nothing like his usual coldness.

"What are you trying to say, my lord?" She realized how tremulous her voice sounded but was powerless to change it.

"I will stand by your side and face down the gossip with you."

Georgia forced a laugh. "Won't that just cause more gossip?"

"Only for a short time. Once you are my countess, they will turn their attention elsewhere."

Thankfully, without her noticing, the dance had ended, because Georgia planted her feet and wrenched out of his arms before turning on her heel and stomping away.

Chapter Fifteen

That wasn't quite the reaction I had been hoping for, Crispin thought drily as he watched the young woman wind her way through the crowded ballroom. He felt the weight of the attention of half the gathered *ton* being divided between himself and Georgia. He realized that his impulsive speech had probably made her situation worse than it had been. He really was turning into a bumbling idiot, he realized with a shake of his head. With a swift glance around the crowded room, he realized he would have to act quickly to stem the flow of trouble he had started.

~~~

Crispin strode down the street. His sense of purpose was faltering the closer he got to his destination. Georgia's reaction to his words the previous evening had not been encouraging. But this was the only way to redeem himself. And he rather thought it would solve several of his problems, including the one where he found he quite liked the girl and couldn't stare into his future without her by his side.

That was the quandary that was making his mission all the more complicated. If he were merely trying to save the girl and her friends from the mess he had created, that carried an almost righteous air to it. But once one brought emotions and feelings into the matter, it was a whole lot bigger pile of horse
~~~

droppings in his mind. *How can I possibly have feelings for her?* he asked himself once again. He didn't even trust her, since she was a woman. Or did he? He had allowed her to push him into contact with his heir, and that had turned out spectacularly well. And the chit was proving to be loyal to her friends. She was willing to leave Town at the height of the Season to spare them any awkwardness. And she was distressed over the dishonesty that had been spread about her. By him, no less!

But none of that mattered, he reminded himself once more. He was here to save the chit from her circumstances. There was much he could provide her. And he was willing to do it. With a firm and renewed stride, he climbed the stairs and rapped soundly on the front door.

A haughty butler opened the door and looked down his nose at him. Crispin had to stifle a grin. It would seem the household had prepared for his arrival.

"Earl Crossley to see Miss Holton, if you please."

"I shall see if she is at home, my lord," the man deigned to say before shutting the door and leaving him outside. Crispin was less amused now. Just as he was about to rap on the door once more, it was pulled open by none other than the object of his visit.

Her cheeks were flushed and her eyes were alight with laughter. "Do come in, my lord. I apologize for the confusion. Some people are quite demonstrative of their feelings."

That statement made Crispin realize the butler's rudeness had been a display of loyalty toward Georgia, and his estimation of her grew even more. If she had managed to instill such feelings in the butler, it said much for her character. But the chit was continuing.

"You should not have been left cooling your heels outside, but I don't think there is much to be accomplished by your visit. I would wish you a good day, my lord."

She was about to dash away. Crispin could feel his jaw wanting to become unhinged. "You couldn't bear for me to be humiliated by being left on the stoop, but you cannot deign to offer me a couple minutes to hear what I have to say?"

She shrugged. "Unless you are here to say you were merely jesting last night, there isn't much to talk about."

"I beg to differ."

Georgia must have realized there were many ears attentive to their conversation. She glanced around at the gathered servants, and even her friend was dawdling on the staircase.

Rolling her eyes and laughing a little, she gestured toward the front room. "Very well, my lord. You can have five minutes to say whatever you think might be important."

Crispin smiled over her long-suffering air. "Your siblings must adore you," he commented.

"Only some of the time," she answered with a smile, catching his joke.

She didn't completely close the door to allow for some propriety, but Crispin figured their voices would be muffled sufficiently as she steered him toward the settee at the far side of the room.

As she took her seat she prompted, "Very well, my lord, what did you have to say?"

Crispin cleared his throat, suddenly nervous as he was finally faced with declaring himself. "I was hoping you could explain why you left in such a way last night."

She stared at him as though he were suddenly speaking gibberish. "Truly, my lord?"

"Crispin," he said. "Could you not call me by my name?"

"No, I could not," she retorted. She continued to stare at him, not answering his first question. Not that he had phrased it as a question, he realized.

He cleared his throat again. "Were you offended by what I said?" he asked gently, nervous that she would say yes.

"Offended? Not precisely, my lord. I would like to think you meant well, but I do not think you need to pay penance for the rest of your life for one mistaken episode of gossip."

She looked so uncomfortable that Crispin was hard pressed not to pull her into his arms. But under the circumstances, that might not be well received. He cleared his throat again and fought the urge to loosen his cravat.

"It would not be penance, my dear. It would be an honour for me to take you as my wife."

She had avoided looking at him for the last minute, but she again brought her gaze back to focus on his face. He was beginning to think the colour in her cheeks was brought by anger if the spark in her eye was anything to go by.

"Really, my lord? You think I will believe that? You think it would be an honour to have me as your wife? You don't even like women very much, let alone trust them. How could you possibly consider having a wife to be an honour?"

Crispin was surprised she had read his feelings so well. He had thought he had hidden them better than that. But then again, he had discussed Christopher's mother with her, so it had probably leaked through.

"I have enough intelligence to be able to discern that you are different from most women. That is one of the things I like most about you." He heard how stiff his voice sounded, but his words were sincere.

Her stare turned pointed as her left eyebrow inched upward. "I don't feel as though you know me at all, my lord. How could you possibly think you have overcome your aversion to marriage sufficiently in such a short amount of time? To me, it seems like the means to make both of us miserable for the rest of our days."

"Do you really think you would find more happiness with whichever shopkeeper you choose from your village to marry?" Crispin's arrogance got the best of him, and he allowed his pique to show.

"I most certainly do. I will bring much of value to such a marriage, my lord. I would feel like a true partner. I know ten pounds means next to nothing to someone like you, but to me and anyone from the village, it is a great deal. With it, my partner and I will be able to build a solid life that will provide for us and my siblings and any other family we might be blessed with."

Her dignity and pride brought a choked feeling to Crispin as he recognized he might not be able to convince her to have him, but in that moment, he realized he would have to persuade her.

"But I could do so much more for your family," he exclaimed.

Her eyes welled with tears. "Monetarily, perhaps, but you forget that I've had the misfortune of witnessing how you treat those in your care. Do you really think I would commit my brothers and sisters to the same fate as Christopher?"

Heat rose in Crispin's face, but he would not allow her words to make him defensive. "That is why I need you to show me the way," he said softly. "You want to be an equal partner in your marriage? You wouldn't get that from me, I'm afraid. You are so much better than me. All I have to offer is my money and title. But you can show me how to live. Me *and* Christopher. I swear to you, I want to do better by the boy, but I haven't a clue where to even start. Except with you. You already showed me the need to start." Crispin tried to explain it to her.

"I spent an hour with him today before coming here. It was awkward at first, but we're finding our way. I told him a little bit about my other holdings. He has only seen Crossley and our London house, but there are others he will need to learn about."

This seemed to catch her attention, and he noticed she was softening her stance toward him. "I told him I would get him a pony. I'm a little cross that his governess hasn't had him riding yet, but I can see that it ought to have been me. You wouldn't believe how excited he was when I promised to teach him to ride."

"Of course, I would believe it. I have two brothers, remember? Even my sisters would probably be excited over a promise like that."

"I could teach them, too, if you'd like."

This brought resistance back into her face, so Crispin continued. "You've showed me how to make a start with Christopher, but I beg of you, show me the rest."

One hot tear spilled over and slid down her cheek. Crispin couldn't bear it. He reached out and wiped it away. She pulled back only slightly. "You needn't marry me for that, my lord. I'd be happy to help you with him. He is a dear boy."

Crispin sensed victory was no longer so far out of reach. He didn't want to frighten her, but he pressed his advantage. "How could we properly get your help if you run back to your village shopkeeper? We will need you nearby to show us how to go on."

He watched as the walls she had erected to hide her feelings began crumbling. She was not so indifferent to him, but her fears were still holding her back.

"What about when he's grown, won't you grow tired of me and wish you had never made such a commitment? Perhaps you just need to hire me as a governess for a time."

"Don't be daft," he whispered softly. "It would be highly inappropriate to do this with the governess," he said as he finally pulled her into his arms. His first brush of her lips was tentative, gauging her reaction. But when she didn't pull away, he pressed for more.

He felt her resistance melting but it was momentary. Much to Crispin's surprise, despite her briefly enthusiastic participation in the kiss, she pulled back. He had to allow her to step out of his arms.

~~~

Georgia crossed her arms to prevent herself from throwing them around him. She had never been so torn in her life. "I have responsibilities, my lord. I cannot so easily allow my head to be turned."

"Crossley is a very large estate, Georgia. I would be happy to have your brothers and sisters there with us."

She lifted her eyebrows at him, trying to keep a barrier of indifference, but it was nearly impossible. She couldn't pretend after kissing him that she didn't care anything for him, but she had to think like a mother, even if she were only a big sister.

"Do you really expect me to believe that in the space of a day you have gone from denying you have a son to being willing to take five children into your heart? Because children need love, my lord. I would not stand for anything less for them."

She refused to be embarrassed by the dawning understanding that seemed to brighten his eyes as he watched her.

"Are you trying to ask about my feelings, Georgia? My feelings about children? Or my feelings about you?"

Georgia kept her arms crossed and her chin high, but she could feel hot colour splashing her cheeks. She couldn't answer him, but she watched him carefully.
~~~

"Perhaps we ought to sit," the earl observed before suiting actions to his words. A lifetime of polite behaviour caused Georgia to sit stiffly beside him.

"I can understand your reluctance to believe me. I have been quite resistant to the thought of remarrying. Up until yesterday, anyway." His tone was gentle, as though he were reciting a well-worn story. Georgia found herself fascinated and relaxed slightly. He continued.

"My wife's riding accident occurred under uncomfortable circumstances. She had luggage with her, and it is understood she was running away from me. From me and her son, in fact. She was a selfish young woman, and I was left with a distaste for any wellborn woman and absolutely no desire to remarry."

Georgia couldn't really blame him for his feelings, but she couldn't allow her brothers and sisters to be put into harm's way despite her urge to try to help him. She had no words so was thankful when he again continued.

"You have made it unavoidably evident that you are nothing like my first wife. Your loyalty to your friends and your siblings sets you apart from any other young woman I've met, but you're in a different world altogether from the sort of woman my wife was. You have forced me to see that I could have a very different life than the one I have been living. And I owe it to Christopher to try to create a family for him."

He grasped her hand and Georgia allowed it. Once more, she felt her resistance melting. Her heart turned over, and she knew it wasn't just his handsome looks that she found attractive. The fact that he would admit to his feelings made her think there was hope for him. This thought brought a trembling smile to her lips, and she watched hope brightening Crispin's face once more.

"I think Christopher could use siblings. If you wouldn't mind lending him yours, I'd be grateful. And I would be delighted to add some younger siblings to the family as well."

Georgia's face flamed at that.

"You are uncharacteristically silent, Georgia," the earl complained, but he had a gentle smile on his face as he did so. "Could you please tell me what you're thinking? I don't know how I can bear to face a future without you. You seemed quite enamored with my son, perhaps you could agree to marry me for his sake."

Finally, Georgia laughed. "Well maybe for his sake, I could consider it."

~~~

Crispin pulled her into his arms but didn't press for more yet. He knew he would frighten her away and needed to be sure of her feelings.

"I promise I'll never treat any children harshly ever again. Not yours, not mine, not ours. Of course, I'll be firm with them if needed, but I swear to you, I'll try to contain my darker feelings in the future."

The expression on her face made his heart soar. Crispin almost shook his head over the ridiculously mawkish thought. *The duke would be thrilled*, was another irrelevant thought that flitted through his head. He squeezed the young woman in his arms.

"Say something, I beg of you. I am declaring myself like a mutton head and telling you I love you, and you can't say anything at all? You normally have more than enough to say."

Georgia finally laughed, but her expression turned reproachful. "Expressing your feelings is *not* mutton headed, Crispin."

Cris was thrilled to hear her use his name for the first time but allowed her to continue.

"But the fact is that you have *not* told me you love me."
~~~

"That has been the point of this entire conversation, my darling girl," he answered.

"You left that part out," she said with another laugh. Finally, she told him what he was desperately waiting to hear. "There's another fact I should add. I've been fighting it since I met you, but I rather think I've fallen in love with you. I didn't want to, you know."

"I know," he answered, squeezing her tighter.

"But it couldn't be helped." She grinned at him. "Oh, the boys are going to be thrilled about the phaeton. Do you really promise to teach them how to drive?"

"I'll teach them everything I know."

"Maybe not everything," she murmured as his head was descending for another toe-curling kiss. He almost stopped to laugh, but now was not the time.

Epilogue

It was the match of the Season.

Rosabel and Hilaria were furious that their little sister's companion was married before they were, but Vigilia was beside herself as she stood up as witness for her best friend.

"Now we can always be together," Vicky sighed with delight.

There had, of course, been the awkwardness about her supposed inheritance, but Crispin had solved that neatly. "We'll just explain that we're tying up your money into dowries for your sisters and any future daughters. I've got more money than people even realize, so I'll set them all up. No one need ever know that there wasn't much of an inheritance to be concerned about."

"But what about my father?"

"He's welcome at Crossley, too."

"But how will we explain his lack of funds?"

"Surely you can learn to look down your nose at people and question why they're asking."

Georgia gurgled with laughter, a common occurrence when they were together. It was a delicious state of happiness that kept her nearly giddy with joy. Crispin hadn't been willing to wait very long to make her his wife. He insisted upon procuring a special license and marrying her at the end of her two weeks as Vicky's companion.

"You can have the two weeks you promised her, but then you're mine," he had said. "I cannot possibly wait any longer than that. In fact, why don't you stay here with her, and I'll go collect your family in the meantime?"

Georgia had stared at him in shock. "Truly? You plan to have them join your household immediately?"

"Why not? You aren't likely to be willing to leave them behind, and I'm not willing to leave you behind."

Georgia was reflecting on all that had transpired in the last fortnight as they made their way out of the city. Crispin had promised they would return shortly, but he wanted to start their new lives on his estate. He had also insisted that all the children ride in a separate carriage.

"I'm eager to learn to share my life with all these children, but riding in a carriage with them is not where I want to start," he had explained firmly.

"I can't believe Lady Sherton was so much help in getting this all organized so quickly," she mused as she leaned on her new husband in the swaying carriage.

"She said it was good practice for the five weddings she has in her future."

"I'm so glad Rosabel finally accepted one of her proposals. Maybe Vicky won't have to wait so very long to find her own match."

"I don't think you need to worry about any of them."

"No," Georgia sighed with a smile. "I think we're all going to live happily ever after."

The End

Now that you've enjoyed Inheriting Trouble,
read the next book in *The Bequest* series:

Courting Intrigue

**Security or loyalty? Attraction or duty?
How does one choose?**

~~~~

To find out what happens with Georgia's friends, the Sherton sisters, download:

A Duke to Elude

**When nefarious schemes threaten her reputation,
he finds his heart on the line with it.**
~~~~

About the Author

I've been writing pretty much since I learned to read when I was five years old. Of course, those early efforts were basically only something a mother could love :-). I put writing aside after I left school and stuck with reading. I am an avid reader. I love words. I will read anything, even the cereal box, signs, posters, etc. But my true love is novels.

Almost ten years ago my husband dared me to write a book instead of always reading them. I didn't think I'd be able to do it, but to my surprise I love writing. Those early efforts eventually became my first published book – Tempting the Earl (published by Avalon Books in 2010). There were some ups and downs in my publishing efforts. My first publisher was sold and I became an "orphan" author, back to the drawing board of trying to find a publishing house. It has been a thrilling adventure as I learned to navigate the world of publishing.

I believe firmly that everyone deserves a happily ever after. I want my readers to be able to escape from the everyday for a little while and feel upbeat and refreshed when they get to the end of my books.

When not reading or writing, I can be found traipsing around my neighborhood admiring the dogs and greenery or travelling the world with my favorite companion.

Stay in touch:

Website/sign up for my newsletter:
www.wendymayandrews.com

Facebook:
www.facebook.com/groups/WMASweetRomanceReadersAndFriends

Instagram:
www.instagram.com/WendyMayAndrews

Twitter:
www.twitter.com/WendyMayAndrews

If you loved this book, check out my two other Regency series:

Book 1 of The Ladies of Mayfair series

The Governess' Debut

The governess must charm both the spoiled child and the haughty earl.

Orphaned and destitute, gently born Felicia Scott must find a way to keep a roof over her head. No longer able to enter the Marriage Mart, but also not of the servant class, the only option is to find a position as governess.

After his spoiled, seven year old daughter has sent off three governesses in the 18 months since her mother died, the Earl of Standish doubts the young, inexperienced Miss Scott could possible manage the position. Since he's desperate and she comes so highly recommended, the earl agrees to give her a chance. Much to everyone's amazement, the beautiful, young governess succeeds where the others had failed. The entire household benefits from the calm, including the jaded earl.

How does he overcome his arrogance to see his governess' true value?

Available now on Amazon

If you like Regencies with a touch of adventure, you will love the Mayfair Mayhem series.

Book 1:

The Duke Conspiracy

Anything is possible with a spying debutante, a duke, and a conspiracy.

Growing up, Rose and Alex were the best of friends until their families became embroiled in a feud. Now, the Season is throwing them into each other's company. Despite the spark of attraction they might feel for one another, they each want very different things in life, besides needing to support their own family's side in the dispute.

Miss Rosamund Smythe is finding the Season to be a dead bore after spying with her father, a baron diplomat, in Vienna. She wants more out of life than just being some nobleman's wife. When she overhears a plot to entrap Alex into a marriage of convenience, her intrigue and some last vestige of loyalty causes them to overcome the feud.

His Grace, Alexander Milton, the Duke of Wrentham, wants a quiet life with a "proper" wife after his tumultuous childhood. His parents had fought viciously, lied often, and Alex had hated it all.

Rose's meddling puts her in danger. Alex will have to leave the simple peace he craves to claim a love he never could have imagined.

Can they claim their happily ever after despite the turmoil?

Available now on Amazon

Made in the USA
Middletown, DE
25 April 2021